ARKANA

The Circle of Nine

Cherry Gilchrist is the author of twelve books, including works on alchemy, astrology and social history. She also works as a professional concert singer, specializing in baroque and Renaissance music, and directs the early music ensemble Arcadia. Cherry was educated at King Edward VI School, Birmingham, and at New Hall College, Cambridge. She was a founder member of both the Saros and the Nine Ladies Associations, organizations concerned with developing the essence of ancient wisdom traditions in the context of modern life. Cherry lives in Bristol with her family, three cats and a dog.

CHERRY GILCHRIST

The Circle of Nine

A NEW MYTHOLOGY OF THE FEMININE

ARKANA

ARKANA

Published by the Penguin Group
Penguin Books Ltd, 27 Wrights Lane, London w8 5tz, England
Viking Penguin, a division of Penguin Books USA Inc.
375 Hudson Street, New York, New York 10014, USA
Penguin Books Australia Ltd, Ringwood, Victoria, Australia
Penguin Books Canada Ltd, 2801 John Street, Markham, Ontario, Canada l3r 1b4
Penguin Books (NZ) Ltd, 182–190 Wairau Road, Auckland 10, New Zealand

Penguin Books Ltd, Registered Offices: Harmondsworth, Middlesex, England

First published by Dryad Press Limited 1988
Published with revisions by ARKANA 1991
1 3 5 7 9 10 8 6 4 2

Printed in England by Clays Ltd, St Ives plc
Filmset in Photina (Monotype Lasercomp)

Contents

Preface

The decision to write this book did not arise in a vacuum, but sprang from work that I have been doing over a number of years with an organization called the Nine Ladies Association. The title of the association is taken from a stone circle of the same name in Derbyshire, near to a residential centre where many courses and working sessions were run by Nine Ladies members. As might be expected, the nine female archetypes described in this book have formed a central theme in the organization's continuing research and teaching programme. Its aim, in general terms, has been to offer women a wider view of life, irrespective of political or religious creed.

The way in which I have set out and interpreted the nine is derived from my own insights and research into their nature. However, their titles, their fundamental qualities and the sense of their significance in human life are all drawn from the teachings of the Nine Ladies Association, to which I give full acknowledgement. The nine female personae have their origins way back in time, although their forms may have changed over the centuries. Likewise, the Nine Ladies teaching organization is said to belong to an ancient tradition of women's work, which has taken on different aspects through the years as the needs and outlook of societies change.

This book is dedicated in general to all who have worked, and all who will work, in the Nine Ladies tradition, and in particular to my daughter Jessica, who will make her own choices.

Cherry Gilchrist
September 1987

Introduction

THE SOURCE OF THE NINE

Each of the nine within time has her form and her custom. Although they are alike, they differ because they are separated, and they stand.

(*Zostrianos*, from *The Nag Hammadi Library*,
edited by James M. Robinson)

When we create a model to explain the world in which we live, we have a choice. The model we make is either on a smaller scale than ourselves, or on a greater scale. The small-scale model is like the world of the microscope, where a sample can be viewed, analysed and described in intricate detail. The larger model is like the realm of star-gazing, horizon-scanning: we look to a bigger reality than the one of the everyday visible world, and measure our human position in these terms. It is a 'large scale' model that I have chosen to use for this book, in describing the feminine psyche. I have taken the premise that each individual life is patterned on, and part of, a bigger scale of life, and that we can glimpse something of its significance through the medium of myth and symbol.

Ultimately, there is only one source of life, and all models and forms of life converge towards this unity. It is the inspiration for them all. In terms of human existence, we can try to fathom the 'blueprint' upon which we are all formed, male and female, but we can also choose to home in upon the different ways in which this human spirit reveals itself in the two sexes. The purpose of this present book is to suggest a model for the feminine psyche, based on the premise that this has its own characteristics, its own identity, as well as being a part of the totality of human life.

I

When I say feminine, I am using the term both in its broadest interpretation and in its individual sense. In other words, the feminine is a principle, an aspect of humanity and of the universe as a whole; it also describes the individual woman, who is a physical representative of that principle. The archetypes used in this book are applied especially to the experience of being a woman today, rather than defining the feminine principle in humanity in general, but it is intended that something of the universal, archetypal feminine may be glimpsed through the models used.

We are all able, as human beings, to invoke both the feminine and the masculine within ourselves. This has been described in psychological terms as the 'animus' and 'anima' within each person – a kind of subterranean male animus lodger in the female, and vice versa. The force of the opposite sex within us is said to give us both the potential for self-realization and also the danger of being possessed by its negative aspects – unwarranted aggression from the animus, for instance, and vanity from the anima.

In the present context, I suggest that this modern interpretation of the duality of each individual can be kept in mind, but that it is not necessarily the only way of understanding the principle of the feminine. The feminine psyche need not be finally defined as being primarily within you, or outside of you. It can be both. In pre-Christian days, it is quite possible that our present understanding was reversed, and that instead of assuming that we are autonomous individuals in possession of certain common basic forces and characteristics, we may very well have seen the great mother goddess, for instance, as the real living power, and humans only as a subservient aspect of her nature. Women becoming pregnant and giving birth would only be manifestations of the goddess, pleasing her with their fertility or attributing their barrenness to her wrath. It is simply another way of looking at things. In approaching the text, which ties together the mythic dimension of life with the familiar, I have therefore tried to keep the field wide open for general interpretation and speculation, while at the same time giving as much practical application as possible, so that the 'nine' are relevant to the lives of women today.

Why describe the feminine psyche through a mythological model? There are three very simple reasons: firstly, myths do not date as quickly as scientific or psychological theories; secondly, they give room for a range of interpretations; and thirdly, they are accessible to everyone, specialist and lay person alike. In the last hundred years we have seen the rise of the specialist society to an extent where it is almost considered essential to have a degree in any subject that you wish to express an opinion on, and the information that comes pouring in through advanced technology can only be deciphered by those with a high level of training. Perhaps this cannot be helped at present, but we still need to find ways to make knowledge accessible to the 'general' person – and that means all of us, since our own specialized area of study does not necessarily equip us to converse with a specialist from another area. The large-scale approach, which I have suggested, is one way of making knowledge generally accessible. Through the use of myth and symbol an arena is created in which we can all meet, communicate and expand our knowledge. Everyone has the ability to connect with myth, and to understand something of its meaning through personal experience of life.

For this particular project, I have set out a series of nine archetypes, each with her own characteristics and symbolism, and I suggest that this circle of nine is one way of representing the totality and the integrity of the female human psyche. The nine have their roots buried deep in the past, yet they are named and described in ways which are relevant to our own time, and possibly to the decades ahead. Myths are immensely adaptable, and are capable of throwing up new truths as we face different challenges during the course of human evolution. Mythical archetypes have a life-form of their own; we can address our questions to them, and see what answers they return. They can give rise to a whole galaxy of stories, and seem to invite us to create new adventures for them. Myths can strike a chord in our own hearts, and we can bring into play imaginative faculties as well as rational ones, when we work with them. Certainly the 'horizon-scanning' approach does not work unless one is prepared to use imagination, emotion and intellect in the quest for truth.

The philosophy of myth is not something that I intend to go into in depth; this book is intended for enjoyable and stimulating reading. I would hope that the reader will find points to add or to argue over, plus other ways of visualizing these archetypes. My aim is to describe these in such a way as to give some insight into their fundamental qualities, but also to leave the way open for other interpretations. In myth there is never one final interpretation; that is its beauty. If this particular model should generate 'small-scale' research, then that too I should welcome, for we need the more specialized, detailed and practical models, and there is a long tradition of scientists and psychologists taking their inspiration from spiritual and symbolical systems of knowledge.

The Nine

Digging deep into mythologies of different ages and cultures, we can find many occasions when nine is the number assigned to women. It probably arises from the root of three – nine being the triple triplicity. The triple goddess is a standard feature of many cultures. There is the triple Hecate, for instance, in classical mythology, herself a representation of the widely known moon goddess who appears in three forms, as the new, crescent and full moon. In some cultures, in ancient Mexico for instance, nine was equally strongly linked with the moon's phases, so that both three and nine are associated with the moon's waxing and waning and the relationship of this to the successive stages of womanhood, of virginity, fertility and barrenness. The triple goddess could be thought of as the raw feminine energy, and the nine as the flowering of this.

This can be traced chronologically in the evolution of the nine Muses, probably the most famous example of the nine in female mythology. They were originally three in number, goddesses first of the springs of water, and then of inspiration; as they became nine, they were known as the Daughters of Memory, and they formed a celestial choir, presenting the gift of prophecy to men and representing the very height of musical and artistic aspiration. Only under Roman culture was each one finally allotted a specific area, such as epic poetry, dance or tragedy, over which to rule. They were not without character though in earlier incarnations; vain and proud, they were incensed when the nine daughters of King Pierus challenged them to a singing competition. Not only did the 'Pierides' lose, but they were changed into magpies for their impertinence. In the evolution from three to nine, there is a parallel in Scandinavian culture, where the Norns, goddesses of destiny, were often numbered as three, and the Valkyries, sometimes known as a company of nine, developed as a group with a more precisely defined role, that of shaping the fate of warriors in battle.

The nine go back still earlier, for there is a cave painting in Catalonia, dating from the Upper Palaeolithic period, which shows nine skirted women dancing around a naked male. Thematically similar is a stone circle in Derbyshire, called 'The Nine Ladies'; this consists of nine stones and a 'male' King Stone placed some way outside the circle, although we cannot be sure at what period the circle was named. In Germanic mythology the wisest of the Gods, Heimdallr, was said to have nine mothers, and in Norse mythology the cult of the goddess Freya included a company of nine seeresses, whose duty it was to travel from place to place offering their services as oracles. Hegir, a god of the sea, had nine daughters, represented by the waves of the ocean, with unpleasant names such as Howler and Grasper. In Celtic mythology, Morgan le Fay is one of the nine sisters of Avalon who bear away the dying King Arthur to tend him with their healing and magic until he appears on earth again; this 'otherworld' was also known as 'The Island of Women'. Nine maidens were said to stir the cauldron of Bran, another Celtic hero, and in medieval Christian iconography the 'Nine Heroines of Christendom' are found.

Historically, interest has been shown in recreating the feminine three and the nine in a cultural context. In Italy, in the late sixteenth century, a group of three singing women, known as the Concerto delle Donne, reigned supreme at the Court of Ferrara. Only the Duke and his most favoured guests were allowed to hear them perform, singing with virtuoso skill in exquisite harmony, and several of those guests hurried away to set up musical imitations of this trio in their own provinces. In this context, nine can be seen as a natural development of three; if there is an upper, middle and lower voice part, and if each lady changes from part to part on different songs, then she takes on a triple aspect, giving the trio a nine-fold means of expression. Bulgarian women commonly sing in groups of three or nine, and when I recently heard such a trio perform, it was fascinating not only to hear the changing combinations of voices, but also to discover how, when they sang as three, they looked and sounded like a unity, as if they represented a modern-day version of the triple goddess herself.

The Circle

Describing the nine as a circle has several useful purposes. Firstly, a circle (as in the Nine Ladies stone circle) can be entered at any point; it has no beginning or end. There is no hierarchy among these archetypes, and one can trace a path between them at will. They can occur in any order in the circle, and the sequence of chapters in this book is purely a personal choice; the chapters could be rearranged to bring out different features of the nine. A female way of working is, basically, non-hierarchical. I do not suggest that this is a 'better' way; women have to learn the need for hierarchy and to use it where appropriate, but their natural inclination is towards equality.

The circle is a good symbol for femininity itself since, physiologically, women are equipped to receive and contain. The straight line is more appropriate for the male. A circle also represents a bounded space, which can be entered and left at will but which provides an area of security, an enclosure which is in itself order rather than chaos. This, too, seems relevant to women, who are often responsible for establishing order and pattern in everyday life, and who seek it amidst the snowstorm of demands that whirls around them.

Male and Female

Writing this book might imply that I must differentiate clearly between male and female characteristics. As far as I can, I shall avoid this hazard! This is partly because I do not think the essence of the feminine is revealed by comparison. Often, the more precise one tries to be in pin-pointing the difference between men and women, the less certain the ground, and the greater the antagonism that can be aroused. Sometimes I have suggested possible basic differences between the two, but, for the most part, I am more concerned to draw on the living source of the feminine, and to describe it in ways which are relevant in contemporary society.

I would like to emphasize yet again that the 'feminine' is human property, not just something understood and owned exclusively by women. Taking my cue from the psychologists, I have already suggested that we all have a link with both sexual principles, and the male readers of this book (of which I hope there are some!) are invited to search for these feminine constellations within their own inner worlds, as well as within the women in their outer lives.

No system of describing the male or female could be complete, however, without reference to the other sex. The suggestion that we can move from a male or female truth, to a human level of truth, and thence to a universal level, implies that we must at some stage assimilate the opposite type of sexual energy and acknowledge it, in order to transcend the apparently divided world of male and female. The myths of the nine, as we have seen, provide for this very well – nine dancers round a male figure, the King Stone, the heroes Arthur and Bran, and the gods Hegir and Apollo. Knowledge of the male must be at the centre of female existence, and vice versa.

Source of the Archetypes

'Archetype' is a much-used word nowadays; it has become a kind of shorthand signifying a quality, a universally recognized myth or symbol which is in some sense bigger than the individual, yet a part of each individual. It provides a link from a personal scale of life to a greater one, which may not only be the 'universal human' but touch on the fundamental structure of created life in all its forms, a 'universal life-form' which transcends and encompasses that of our own particular, human species.

The psychologist C. G. Jung, who was largely responsible for the adoption of this concept into present-day thinking, defined an archetype in its purest state as being empty and formless in itself, like the axial system of a crystal which has no material form of its own, but around which the crystal can grow. The crystal itself is similar to the form with which we, through conscious experience, give recognizable structure to the archetype. These formulations that we create help us to a better understanding of the more abstract, larger-scale realm that lies beyond them, as well as the meaning of everyday experience.

In this book, nine archetypes will be described, and I shall refer to their names and forms as 'archetypes', even though, strictly speaking, an archetype is beyond such a description. And, although in this context, the nine female archetypes have been given human form and characteristics, it is important to recognize that they are not the same as individual people. They are personifications of aspects of the feminine psyche, which itself is a 'universalized' form of the individual psyche. We have these archetypal qualities and energies within us, and they can be described in images which may make it easier for us to recognize them and attune ourselves to them. But it would be unwise to identify with them completely. An archetype is, in a sense, 'non-human'; the individual human is a cluster of archetypes, or fundamental traits, imbued with further essential qualities, such as will and love. Something recognizably archetypal can emerge in a person when he or she takes on a role or image that magnifies certain characteristics – and thus are born heroes, heroines, film stars, charismatic leaders, and so on, as well as villains and fanatics. But the archetype is not the whole person. In fact, for everyone there are times when one archetype or another reveals its hovering presence, but it does not usually take over your personal life, even though its effects can be powerful.

In general terms, we blend and distil the energies that the archetypes represent, and use them in moulds of our own making. The nine female archetypes are described here in a way which I hope will make them seem real and relevant to our lives, and to this end I shall use many mundane examples of how their qualities can manifest themselves. This is the interpretation, the illustration, but the figure herself is less clearly definable. She can shrug off the set of associations in which I have clothed her, and appear in another time and place in different costume.

I shall also hope to provide inspiration for how we can call upon and use the qualities of these archetypes in our own lives, rather than simply allowing them to operate behind the scenes, as it were. It is possible to make more choices when we can recognize the influences that are moving us; we may choose to emphasize or diminish the force of an archetype, to channel it in more constructive ways, or to call upon its power in time of need.

I assume that each woman has something of all these nine within her; they give her completeness, totality. However, there is somewhere further to go, beyond the domain of the feminine, as the 'King Stone' principle points out, and therefore, although we can recognize and develop the archetypal qualities within us, we should not allow them to have absolute power over us.

The Three in the Nine

The set of nine is made up of three Queens, three Ladies and three Mothers. Thus within the circle there is a triple root, as with the tradition of the triple goddess. This suggests three modes of being, which we might describe as the containing, the releasing, and the integrating (see also p. 164). The containing holds energy in, the releasing lets it expand outward, and the integrating – naturally enough – integrates it. People may act predominantly in one of these three ways. There are those who contain their responses, holding in the power of their feelings. There are those whose tendency is to react spontaneously, and never keep anything back, and then again there are those who will weigh up impressions, and allow themselves to be changed by the process. We can see these same three forces working in ourselves: an idea comes into your head, and first of all you embrace it enthusiastically. The next day, however, you are full of doubts; there are pitfalls you had not thought of, and it all seems a little crazy. But after that you reach a state where you can weigh all this in the balance. The initial ardour may be tempered, but if it is, basically, a good idea then you can see now that the drawbacks are not so very great and that it is worth proceeding with. The third state, the balancing out, has a quality of its own, rather than being just a mixture of the other two. At this point you may have quite a new vision of the original idea and it may have a solidity which the first rush of enthusiasm lacked. So these forces are fundamental to the human psyche; in describing them as Mother, Queen and Lady, I am looking at their feminine aspects. However, there is a tradition of associating them with the feminine, as examples of the triple goddess cited above show, and in the Judaic tradition the three letters Aleph, Mem and Shin are known as 'The Three Mothers'. Here we are using the terms Mother, for the containing, Lady, for the releasing, and Queen for the integrating, or unifying.

These terms may provoke question, since they each have connotations which can affect us quite intensely. Lovers of history and mythology may find the terms Queen and Lady to their liking, whereas those whose eyes are firmly fixed on the world of today may find these words old-fashioned or misleading. Those who welcome motherhood may be quite at ease with the appellation of 'Mother', but women who want to sidestep that role may feel less happy with the word. There are both personal and cultural associations in operation; in literal terms, today, mothers are very plentiful, whereas queens are thin on the ground, and lady is a title with very ambivalent qualities. It has become identified with 'class' and 'breeding' and artificial manners, although originally it suggested a true refinement of the feminine principle.

If we are to go as deeply into the realm of myth and archetype as possible, then it is helpful to go beyond our initial surface response to words. Ultimately, one of the purposes of myth is to give us a deeper sense of meaning and pattern in life. We have more chance of seeing that if we are willing to drop some of our own patterns of association, which limit our vision. The names and terms used in this book are not the only ones that could be used; they are a set which have proved to be both useful and evocative, and the reader is invited to consider them in context, and see whether they can be illuminating.

As the nine archetypes are described, so these three basic terms will become clearer, but to begin with, a few pointers can be given:

The Queens represent female figures who act as centres of life. They know how to be, how to maintain, how to draw towards themselves what they need. They are symbols of presence and confidence; they have a domain over which they rule. In the body, they could be said to symbolize the heart.

The Mothers are the rulers of structure and order. They create a space, and receive within it, protecting and enclosing. They understand the laws of time and space, and from their knowledge make forms and patterns. They take what is necessary to further growth, and reject the rest. Their physical symbol is the womb.

The Ladies are the active energies, doing and giving. They know how to create flow out of that which is static. They have grace and poise. They can handle change with ease. They are able to turn base, unpromising material into something that has lightness and charm. They can be represented by the physical 'aura', the halo of energy that permeates and surrounds the body.

The Nine in Our Time

Our current mythologies are fragmented. We have become aware of the need to retrieve symbolic insights into life, but in many cases – as with alchemy, or classical mythology – these are hard to recapture in their entirety. I would hope that this circle of nine, a model of the female psyche, provides a whole way of knowledge, and that it can be understood both in its specific descriptions and as a totality. Cults of the past have tended to lean towards one or another of these female archetypes – there have been contexts where a 'Goddess of Love' or of 'Fury' has reigned supreme, for instance. It seems that we have lost sight of the totality of the feminine, and that we need to re-establish it, and understand it, so that we can draw from it the elements we particularly need to help us through current and future years.

The Nine in the Future

Launching this set of nine is like sending a boat into unknown waters. We can only guess what may lie ahead for us – men and women going into space, and perhaps colonizing other planets in ways which would seem alien to us if we could visualize them now. Even in the last ten years, technology has advanced at a rapid rate and many things are possible now which were not only a decade ago. Some advances immediately open up possibilities, while others pose enormous ethical problems. We need both creativity and responsibility to meet the changes that are taking place.

It may be that this 'boat' carries nothing of use to a future, changed world. On the other hand, it is possible that the mythological framework will have within it that which goes beyond the present cultural conditioning; and that it will still be used as a guide to the essential female nature, and may even suggest practical ways in which a balanced and enjoyable life can be established in new circumstances. If this should be so, then the reader of the future is invited to take the kernel, and throw away the husk – every set of symbols has to be reinterpreted at different periods.

Reading this Book – a Magical Journey

I have suggested that the circle of nine can be set up in any sequence, and that it can be travelled in any order. Therefore, I have written this book so that you may make your journey through chapters 1–9 in whichever order you like. You may take an obvious route, such as reading about all the Queens, then all the Mothers, then the Ladies, or devise a sequence of your own. Each journey creates its own story. In each chapter, you see the world from the particular vantage point of the female archetype under consideration; when you move on, the world changes. When you have completed your pathway through the nine, then you have seen the feminine from every viewpoint, and can appreciate its totality.

The Portraits

At the end of each chapter, a portrait is given of the figure just described. The headings used are designed to draw its characteristics together, and to provide a form of cross-reference between different chapters. They may also help to give a more condensed version of the archetype which can tie into personal experience and associations.

The first section of each portrait is called 'Images'. These are designed to show three types of image which the archetype may acquire. The first, the street image, is a light-hearted look at how one might encounter this goddess walking down the road in modern dress. The second, the mythic, is more symbolic and based on mythology and cultural associations. The third, the personal, is rather like holding up a mirror; it suggests where we can find the archetype operating in our own lives.

The second section, 'Evolution', takes us through the youth, maturity and old age of the figure. As with the images, these are only examples, which may serve to stimulate portraits of your own. The terms are not used with any fixed span of years in mind; sometimes the description of youth seemed more appropriate to girlhood, sometimes to adolescence or young womanhood, for instance.

The third section, called 'Manifestations', looks at the appearances these archetypes make in our lives, through the gifts and trials they send us, and the rituals and cults by which we honour them. Examples may well seem more mundane and less grandiose than this suggests, but it is worth looking at many everyday activities and seeing the buried elements of ritual that lie there. A ritual or cult is something more than the mere servicing of physical needs; in one sense it is a magical activity that serves emotional or spiritual purposes too. Many activities that we carry out without thinking have something of this at their heart.

Gifts and trials are interesting to consider, for a gift may not always be a blessing, and a trial proves to have real value. The old saying, 'Be careful what you ask for, because you may get it' is relevant; it is a fascinating exercise to ask yourself what three gifts you would like to receive, and then to think through the consequences, and to think again whether you really wish to be blessed with them. The trials cited may be ones of deprivation or of overwhelming influences; both seem to have validity in this context.

The 'Vision' is the fundamental source of life which gives rise to the archetype, and takes us beyond the realm of the feminine to that of universal life.

Prologue

THE CIRCLE

It is night. The stone circle lies deep in shadow. The space within it is heavy and dark, and the stones are no more than brooding shapes, leaning into an unfathomable abyss. They are sensed rather than seen; their number is elusive, their contours glimpsed then lost like the edges of a remembered dream. And then the moon breaks through the dense cloud. The light touches the stones. They are in focus; their number is nine. Gnarled cracks run over them, caught sharp in the moonlight. Fissures deepen, surfaces gleam. Gone is the stillness; the stones seem alert, alive. Their strange shapes twist until the figures become fluid, soft and mobile. The Nine are released from their frozen posture, for the light has touched them again and the eye that sees them acknowledges their being.

In this cool light of night, their forms seem to grow and change in a thousand ways until at last the eye holds them in view, and their features are mirrored in the imagination.

There is one who is never still. Stars spark from her fingers, and her hair flows like water as she dances, light-footed, on the dewy grass. The breeze tosses her; she springs, leaps and turns, her dress billowing and silken around her. She is incorrigible, joyful, irresistible.

The Just Mother remains in shadow, still brooding, but she is ready and awaits the moment. Her cloak is black, but her sword is silver, keen and poised. Her features are strong, and sad, for she cannot forget what she knows.

15

Round, apple-cheeks and laughing. You may laugh too, if you please, for she is the fat of the earth, pleased with life, glad to be there. There is mud upon her feet, but on her head a royal crown of corn; a harvest of fruit spills from her hands.

Where there was a stone, there now seems to be a hollow, scooped out, with a warm fire gently burning there. The one in blue tends it, the Lady of the Hearth. She is preparing for guests, strangers, and those who will come after. The work is done quietly, and few realize the constancy of her attention. Be welcome, traveller; be seated and tell your tale.

She whose shape is never formed. She, warm and heaving, the rough lump of stone brought to life and pulsing like gushes of dark blood in the veins. Some call her the Great Mother, for she always contains; however great the shape within, she is greater still. Respect and fear gather round her, for she is first and last.

Brilliant in moonlight, keen as a cat, wild as an owl, swift as the winged horse. The Queen of the Night greets her court, the darkness surrounding her charged, electric. She will wait for no one, cannot be halted. She raises her hands and arms; her hair streams behind her as her cloak glistens, flapping and beating like a great bat.

The Lady of Light is a silken gleam, a muted outline, a lamp of peace. In her fullness of light she becomes no-thing, no one, and to see her shape you must veil her splendour. She is always there, the one who never goes, even in the dead of night. Her light touches like the warmth of the sun; stillness and movement are one to her.

Rolling the spindle between her hands, teasing out the thread, the Weaving Mother is thoughtful. She has no hurry; purpose is not rushed. Her hands are quick and deft, her eyes practised and steady. Now her fingers run through the threads, straightening them for the work that is to come, a tapestry of patterns and colours without number.

The most beautiful one. Cheeks like satin stretched over ivory. Gold and silver, glittering in her robes. You see her as a tiny, perfect blue flower of spring. As a cascading waterfall. As a finely cut crystal. You will see her as your image of beauty, contained, radiant, of the essence.

These are the Nine, keeping the circle. Let us meet them one by one.

1

The Queen of Beauty

The Many Faces of Beauty

It is dawn. A soft, golden light has spread across the sky, like a luminous cloud risen above the rounded hills. The shadows are wisps of grey, green and blue, a delicate veil over distance, muffling substance and smoothing the valley textures. There are small ripples, wind-blown, on the lake, where the water catches the first flashes of brilliance from the early sun. The scene is both ancient and utterly new. It heralds the day, clear-washed, infinite in possibility. Its hints and mysteries draw the spirit, as enticing as its revelations.

As the day progresses, it changes. In the heat of noon the eye rests on single details, so great is the glare of the sun. Small blue harebells, and brilliant yellow gorse, smelling of warm coconut. Rocks burning to the touch, cushioned with furry moss. On the lake, pleasure boats, each its own world of colour, words and movement. The landscape is as simple, naïve and charming as a child's painting.

Towards the end of the afternoon, however, it changes again. A wind gets up, clouds gather, and the sky has darkened. Rain lashes down, so that the lake spits and bubbles like a cauldron. The hills loom heavily through the storm, single trees tossed and drenched by the downpour. There is a sombre majesty in the scene. As colour fades, so an immensity of scale is revealed where the inhospitable water stretches away to the forbidding height of the hills.

Which of these three visions showed the true beauty of the

landscape? Was one more real, more beautiful, more significant than another? As individual beholders, we may have found more meaning in one of the views than in others. It may have evoked a response in our personal nature, or have been in keeping with the mood of the moment. Yet each vision arose from the same landscape, and each had its own particular beauty and power.

The Queen of Beauty has many faces; beauty is not fixed. It is more like a gemstone which has been cut and faceted, so that each way it is turned shows a different angle, catching the light in a thousand different ways. Women do not have the one way in which to be beautiful, but many. The Queen of Beauty cannot be pinned down to one expression, and every female image of beauty that is created is only a single realization of a great range of possibilities. Societies and fashions change; an ideal of beauty is pictured, embellished, explored, and then released in favour of another. In this century alone we have had a succession of such images, from the stately, big-busted, Edwardian beauty, through the languid and willowy pre-Raphaelite heroine, the boyish 1920s 'flapper', the sleekly groomed, wide-shouldered 1940s woman of the world, to the innocent, long-haired nymph of the 1960s and the colourful gypsy of the 1970s. All over the world, standards of beauty vary; fat women can become the ideal, or those with small feet, or tall women, or those with blue eyes, or whatever it is that seems to capture the spirit of beauty for a particular time and place.

It is appropriate that the image of beauty should not be fixed. Each image has something different to convey, and opens up a new range of aesthetic possibilities, and as beauty itself can move and inspire us, so different images can awaken new emotions within us. It is appropriate, too, because women themselves are subject to changes of image and form. Cycles of growth and childbearing produce markedly different states of appearance in women. A pregnant woman is very obviously a different shape from her non-pregnant sister, and the beauty of a young girl has quite another quality from that of a mature woman. Even during the monthly menstrual cycle an individual woman's image may change: subtle differences are produced in complexion, expression and posture, differences which the woman may choose to emphasize in her dress according to her state of mind and body.

The Queen of Beauty encompasses the ebb and flow of feminine life, and she represents the possibility of expressing each nuance of this. Beauty is not fixed, or frozen, even though we have our preferred modes for expressing it. Societies may choose to emphasize the 'fecund' side of the feminine, by exalting an image of woman that is plump and heavy-breasted, or there may be a preference for a youthful, virginal beauty, with 'natural' styles of hair and a slim figure to go with it. The individual woman must somehow find her own approach to beauty, an image which is likely to be influenced by cultural expectations, by her own natural attributes, her personality, and by her current stage of life. She creates her own sequence of images within the larger social context. Even the woman who detests fashion or 'artificial' aids to beauty will still create an image, and even the perception of 'ugliness' can still fall within the realm of the Queen of Beauty, for beauty is not just that which is lovely, and charming, but includes much more.

Beauty Within, Beauty Without

Does beauty spring from the inner self, or from the outward physical form? This question is a rose with not a few thorns; women do not like the assumption often made by men (especially poets) that the beautiful face describes an equally beautiful soul. It becomes oddly insulting, not only because it rules out appreciation of beautiful souls lurking behind plain faces, but also because the kind of admiration then given to the beautiful woman begins to assume that her equally lovely nature is sweet, kind, gentle and unselfish – an image of passive, yielding femininity. Such an image ignores other characteristics of women – their strength, wit, skill, energy and anger, for instance. It can lead to a perpetual and escalating attempt by women to please, trying to retain their outward beauty at all costs, and to show only the lovely, pleasing side of their nature for fear that they will otherwise be dethroned. Keeping up permanent co-ordination between personality and outer appearance is as oppressive as never daring to appear in public without a set of fully matching clothes and accessories.

There is a link between outer and inner beauty, but it is not rigid; it is a changing balance, a flow operating between the two. Nor are they necessarily equal in strength; the outer form may be more compelling than inner character, or vice versa. For the observer, perhaps real beauty is known when the soul can be recognized in the features of the face, and the form of the body. Perhaps, too, there are times in each woman's life when that harmony is most apparent. Love may light up beauty; falling in love, holding a new baby, even the compassion and tears that come with bereavement can create an aura of beauty around a woman that reflects the deep emotions of the soul. And what price fashion and make-up then?

If physical beauty and internal beauty are not the same, even though they are linked, then instances may occur when one or the other is almost totally absent. The effect of a strong inner beauty, with no outward form, for example, can be both powerful and disturbing. It reveals a primitive beauty springing from the very roots of the feminine, a true nakedness of the inner woman. In his wanderings through India, Miguel Serrano found himself arrested by a grotesque sight in the streets of Delhi:

One day I saw a man pulling a small cart. This cart had wheels, and inside it was a small thing, a body without legs, nothing more than a naked bust with arms that stopped at the wrists. It was a woman. Her breasts were eaten with leprosy and so was a part of her face. Her hair was disorderly, and the color of her skin was bluish black, which is a sign of incurable leprosy. Nevertheless, she had deep and peaceful eyes, and when she passed me by she only smiled; she asked me for nothing. But that smile was so tremendous, and so feminine, that I confess I felt an attraction for that thing, that woman-thing. The essence of the feminine spirit was still there, untouched by the ravages of her leprosy.

(Miguel Serrano, *The Serpent of Paradise*, Routledge & Kegan Paul, 1974)

When I was at school, we used to take it in turns to visit a former pupil, a woman in her twenties, who lay in hospital incurably handicapped. She was said to be the most handicapped person in Britain at that time, since, due to a rare muscular disease, she was paralysed throughout her whole body except in her big toe. The effects of this on her appearance were utterly disastrous; without muscle tension her face had become a near-shapeless mass, down which mucus and saliva coursed. Her toe was rigged up to a bell, and she would ring this, using a number code to spell out messages, and by this means she was thus able to communicate her needs, and keep up some sort of conversation.

Nowhere in her physical being was there any last trace of beauty. In fact, in an attempt to compensate for this, the nurses would paint nail varnish on her toe-nails and put bows in her hair. Well-meant though it was, the gesture was terrible, creating a ghastly parody of femininity. But, as with Serrano's 'woman-thing', something came through. She could laugh, and though no sound came out, you could see her shaking. She spelt out jokes by using the bell, and loved to be read to. The essence of her nature could still express itself and be known by her visitors, and it was in this quality of spirit that her last claim to beauty lay. I think all of us who visited her were strongly affected by her situation, and it was an early lesson in finding out what survives when all the outward normalities of life are stripped away.

At the other extreme there are women who have devoted themselves to perfecting physical beauty. Such beauty may make a strong impact, but, if it has little relationship with the inner nature, it is precarious. Of a beautifully groomed, heavily made-up woman it was once said: 'It looks as though you could peel her face off.' Beauty intensified in this way can become rigid, artificial, unbelievable. If you were to strip off the face, like a rubber mask, what would be underneath? The images created by photographic and fashion models and by 'beauty queens' are vulnerable in the same way. All the trappings of a lovely figure, clothes, make-up and hair-style can create a vivid, sharply focused image, but one that is better on the pages of a glossy magazine or on the television screen than in real life. Such images have little flexibility and may easily be destroyed by mundane realities. Can the model tuck into a hamburger and chips in her lunch break and still keep that sultry look? What will happen to the smiling pose of Miss World when she comes down with a cold?

The Realm of Physical Beauty

Not all women consider themselves to be beautiful, or indeed wish to be so in conventional terms. But every woman makes a choice about her appearance; she is exercising the power of the Queen of Beauty, which is to express qualities of being through the physical medium. We choose to be attractive, or dowdy, to enhance what nature has given us or to play it down; we can dress in a way that we feel accords with our essential character or choose to create a fantasy image which bears little resemblance to the personality. There is no fixed scale of 'right or wrong' here; we respond to the demands of different occasions, different phases of our lives and to changing moods and drives within the psyche. But choose we do, and any one of those choices can turn out to be effective and appropriate, or not. If you go to a fancy-dress party as a Turkish dancer, you can expect a good time; if you travel on public transport late at night in such a get-up it will probably cause nothing but trouble.

The pursuit of physical beauty has caused women much enjoyment, amusement, frustration and excitement through the centuries. Fashion and make-up have been with us for a very long time indeed – there are make-up palettes surviving from ancient Egypt – and although men in certain times and cultures may devote a lot of effort to their appearance, it has remained chiefly a feminine domain. Physical appearance is a more vital medium of expression for women than for men; men may like to adorn and admire themselves, but in the last analysis, when something more interesting comes along – adventure, challenge, war – they will drop any interest in appearance, for it is an optional extra. They will go for uniform, very often, whether it's the business man's suit or military gear. Perhaps uniform is itself more a male-inspired phenomenon. It enforces collectivity, smooths the edges of masculine individuality, welds together the team. Women, on the other hand, have no trouble in sensing their collectivity; it is their individuality that they strive to bring out, and demonstrate through appearance. Girls in school uniform, women in hospital nightgowns, mothers struggling with poverty, who have no time or money to spend on their appearance, can feel that they are being depersonalized. Women may sense that their own nature is being violated when any choice in personal appearance is taken away from them.

What happens in the pursuit of physical beauty? During a visit to the hairdresser's I realized that we women are prepared to put ourselves through the most extraordinary practices in order to improve our image. Physical beauty has initiation processes, taboo areas, indignity, ridiculousness and suffering. On this occasion, we had come to place ourselves under the authority of the hairdressers, to cast ourselves upon their mercy since, with the snip of the scissors, our dreams could be realized or ruined. We allowed them to see us at our most absurd. Women sat with clips holding up large chunks of hair, with peculiar rubber caps over their heads through which little wisps of hair were teased, with rollers over their whole scalps looking like a perverted kind of cactus. Nor was I exempt, being plastered with a particularly smelly preparation, which would look to those not in the know like ripe cow dung. All of us would arise in due course like Venus from the waves – shining, lovely, renewed, with sharp neat cuts, elegant waves or subtle highlights – or so we hoped; it was an act of faith.

The handmaidens of the Queen of Beauty – servants, perhaps I should say, since many of them are men – know their own power. Shy young hairdressing assistants rapidly become bold and cheeky after a few months of work. Dress shop assistants grow supercilious, aware that they can uplift or slay us with a single comment. When our appearance is being changed – in the hairdresser's, beauty salon or fitting room – there is great vulnerability, and if we ask for assistance we are giving others considerable power to judge us, alter us and witness us stripped of normal dignity. Only the hairdresser sees our grey hairs when the dye is out, or knows about the dandruff problem. The shop assistant may glimpse the bulges that we conceal so cleverly, and the beauty parlour attendant get a close-up of nasty blackheads and facial hair.

As I have suggested before, creating and enhancing beauty is a tricky business, for if a woman endeavours to obliterate all flaws, weathering and odd characteristics, she makes herself very vulnerable, for it is easy then to break the illusion. It is an art to bring out the best without telling a visual lie. The seventeenth-century poet Robert Herrick thought that a little carelessness in appearance was actually very exciting:

DELIGHT IN DISORDER

A sweet disorder in the dress
Kindles in clothes a wantonness:
A lawn about the shoulders thrown
Into a fine distraction:
An erring lace, which here and there
Enthrals the crimson stomacher:
A cuff neglectful, and thereby
Ribands to flow confusedly:
A winning wave, deserving note,
In the tempestuous petticoat:
A careless shoe-string, in whose tie
I see a wild civility:
Do more bewitch me than when art
Is too precise in every part.

The Axis of Beauty

It is clear by now that in the realm of beauty we are working with polarities – conflicts and tensions, which force the individual to make a conscious choice about her image. It is rather as though there is a central axis, around which the gemstone of beauty is formed. Its poles represent those issues and challenges, all of which are in the province of the Queen of Beauty. There are the polarities of inner and outer beauty, of age versus youth, of sexual and transcendent beauty, of beauty concealed and beauty revealed, of fantasy and reality, and of charm and ugliness. Every archetypal principle contains opposing characteristics within itself; this is why such archetypes can be dynamic and provide possibilities of growth. The beautiful and the hideous are part of the same principle. The Queen of Beauty cannot be truly beautiful, and have known and understood beauty, unless she has realized ugliness too. Beauty that denies its opposite becomes shallow and artificial.

Consistently keeping up an outward appearance of beauty can be a strain, and even a repression of other forces which need expression. A permanently lovely, exquisite and gracious Queen of Beauty could become irritating; indeed, to be enthroned as a 'beautiful woman' in the mind of a male admirer can be a horrible experience. We need to retain the choice to present ourselves to the world as 'not-beautiful', to prevent suffocation and keep up a satisfactory interaction with people and tasks that we encounter. Take the custom of mourning, for instance; at the funeral itself, and traditionally for a much longer period, a woman who has lost a husband or close relative wears black, and can be thus almost anonymous in appearance. She is released from the obligation to look good. And if a woman is tackling strenuous, dirty, physical tasks, she does not want to bother about presenting a pleasing picture; clothes suitable for the job are a priority above a glamorous image. She need not rely for her sense of identity upon outward appearance; she may in fact look beautiful, she may look a mess; it does not matter greatly at that particular time. Confidence in the feminine within allows us to let go of the outer image from time to time.

Sometimes a mood, or a phase of the menstrual cycle, will bring about a definite aversion to keeping up appearances. An elegance which was enjoyed only a few days earlier can now seem artificial, out of touch with the sense of self that has arisen. Such a change can be positive, giving a breathing space and a chance not to become too fixed in outward images. It can also be a sign of darker moods and feelings surfacing, the need to be angry, defiant, or isolated. For many women, these feelings will come and go and the physical appearance is a useful barometer which the husband, boyfriend or employer will learn to read, if he is wise. Some women can become fixed in the 'negative pole' expression of image, however; just as a woman can wear a rigid mask of beauty, so too she can go to the opposite extreme and deliberately make herself ugly in order to protect herself and demonstrate her anger against the world, or, possibly, her dislike of men. Allowing oneself to be beautiful is, after all, risky; it brings response, and gives something to live up to. But the cult of ugliness can become just as fake as the cult of prettiness if it is a denial of its opposite.

Women expose themselves through their image far more than men do. Even though the image is, to some extent, chosen and contrived, it tends to highlight genuine individual characteristics, and, like it or not, a woman is judged by her image. Feminine image and identity are connected, and we are vulnerable and concerned about personal appearance. It is therefore understandable that very many taboos and prohibitions have developed around physical exposure, whether it is bodily nakedness or attending to personal grooming. What is, and what is not, permissible varies with time and place. At one school I attended for a short while, very much for 'young ladies', the headmistress descended unexpectedly on a class, with a visitor, and found it in uproar. In the icy post-mortem, held in assembly the following day, the greatest crime we were condemned for was not the shouting and shrieking, but the fact that: 'One gal was sitting on her desk *combing her hair*!' Outmoded this view might be, but most of us would still prefer to try on new clothes, wax hair off our legs, perform our ablutions or put on make-up in private. We would like – wishful thinking perhaps – there still to be some apparent magic in the way we renew and transform our outward image. Some of the myths surrounding the goddess Venus warn that the worst trespass against her is to see her naked and asleep.

Beauty and Character

The face of a young child asleep is very beautiful. It is innocent; cleared of all the expressions that the child has been trying out during the day. The artlessness of babyhood is still there. Young girls, before they reach adolescence, have an instinctive grace in their movements. Even though they may already be thinking about their appearance, and becoming fashion-conscious, on many occasions all this is forgotten and, in running, dancing or laughing, they revert to a natural ease through which a certain innocence shines. As they grow, the 'natural' option becomes less and less available. Not only do adolescents start self-consciously considering every square inch of their outward appearance, but their personalities and habits begin to be printed there too. Sometimes the image they create may be a long way from expressing their real character but the search is on – through fashions, chats with friends, reactions from boyfriends – to find a style that suits their temperament and physical type.

There is no return to the innocence of childhood. As women mature, their outward appearance becomes more and more strongly related to character. Denials of this are glaringly obvious; a 'little-girl' look cannot hide the marks of experience on the face of a middle-aged woman, lines which will reveal good or bad humour. In youth it is relatively easy to create a physical beauty, while the character is still not fully formed; later on, the search for beauty seems to take on a different aspect, that of expressing the true individual femininity in the most appropriate way. Not every woman takes up that challenge. Some, as mentioned, cling to youthful appearance and risk looking absurd. Others give in, decide that they are past the stage where beauty has any relevance, and concentrate, perhaps with relief, on merely looking tidy and presentable. Of those who try to retain their former beauty, some apparently succeed very well, but without really allowing age and experience to modify this. In several instances I have observed women successfully give an impression of being about ten years younger than they really are, until a major event happens in their lives, a death in the family perhaps, or a divorce. The shock can have a sudden and lasting effect; the woman's energy is no longer channelled into her appearance, and it seems as if she has made up the extra ten years, and more, all at once.

Each woman has to make a choice as to how she expresses the ageing process. The focus of beauty gradually shifts from the physical body to the inner nature. And yet the physical medium can still radiate something that is attractive, beautiful even, although it is no longer 'beautiful' in conventional terms. The eyes, the expressions of the face, posture, gesture and quality of movement can all convey beauty at any age. This may be an art that we need to rediscover, since in modern society the positive attributes of age are usually ignored, the cult of youth being dominant. There are signs that this is happening. The strongest youth cultures of the century were in the 1950s and 1960s, and now that the members of this generation are over the border into middle age, they are showing an egotistical, but maybe quite a healthy reluctance to let go of the limelight. There are the obvious queens of health and beauty cults for the older woman, such as Jane Fonda, Callan Pinkney (of Callanetics fame) and Joan Collins. Less extreme examples can be found in any street or office, and there is a move among women to make the best of 'prime-time', a phase which has been described as the years between 35 and 60, the time when a woman can capitalize on her experience, energy, and maturity. This seems to correspond to a refusal to sink into dowdiness, a drive to develop a new image of beauty and good looks appropriate to this particular stage of life. As we grow older, who we are will be more and more clearly etched in our appearance, but we can use this positively and work with it, rather than against it.

The Archetype of Beauty

To be beautiful is a responsibility. The face of Helen of Troy is said to have launched a thousand ships, and the beauty of Cleopatra created havoc in the Roman Empire. Beauty itself has been declared through the ages to be an exalted physical state, hinting at qualities of light, grace and love whose source lies beyond the material world and yet which can enter into physical substance and transform it. Physical beauty has long been seen as a reflection of God's presence in the world; mystical texts describe the divine beauty to be found in creation as the female spirit, the bride and the beloved. The ultimate 'aim' of beauty, if there can be said to be such a thing, is to point us towards the spiritual realm. And it may be that there are certain women whose beauty is so strong, so close to the archetype of the Queen of Beauty, that they produce an intense effect upon other human beings. If such a woman is not capable of handling the feelings and energies she arouses, then the results may be catastrophic, of life-and-death proportions.

Public longing for such an idol of beauty may help to create temporary goddesses, seen in the popular eye as representatives of the Queen of Beauty. Film stars, such as Marilyn Monroe, are likely candidates, and the pressure of such a role can create unbearable conflict; Monroe killed herself at an early age and at the height of her popularity. Royal women, too, even though quite ordinary in appearance, may be elevated in public opinion until they are considered to be the utmost in charm and elegance – again difficult to live up to, when they are continually 'on show'.

The English came very close to establishing a real live Queen of Beauty in the person of Elizabeth I; her cult was that of the ever-lovely and ever-youthful Virgin Queen. Her name was linked to the goddess Diana, and her qualities praised almost to the level of the Virgin Mary, whose glories she was meant to replace in newly Protestant England. She had to keep up this act until well into old age; there was a tacit understanding that her decline should be ignored, and that poems, tributes and honours of all kinds should still be heaped upon her as though she were a beautiful young Princess. Although her popular image was contrived, it served the whole nation, inspiring art, literature, music and pageantry. Through the creation and maintenance of that image, she gave access to a particular source of energy, to a kind of mythology that fed the life of the court and country, uniting her realm under a common symbol and filling it with colour and vitality. It would be wrong to assume that Elizabeth's reign was one of perfect happiness and freedom, or that the contrast between her real physical state and her royal image was not sometimes ridiculous. But it was an option chosen and sustained by the Queen herself, her government and her people, and the power of such a symbol produced a great flowering of culture and a sense of national identity that has perhaps not been surpassed since.

Elizabeth herself was not the archetype, nor can any single living human being be an archetype in his or her own right. The Queen of Beauty is more than one view or expression of beauty. It is strange to see, however, how a 'supra-personal' quality can be hinted at in a girl or woman, coming close to the archetypal spirit. In the street, or on the train, you may glimpse a face that seems to be that of a Greek goddess, an African queen, or a Renaissance angel. Only if you look more closely do you notice where the image falls short. Your goddess, perhaps, is chewing gum. Your queen has a nasty way of scratching her nose, and your angel is in a sulk. For such a quality to be fully present, body, psyche and spirit would all have to be of that higher order. In nearly every case, what is seen is a hint of something that could be, but is not. Beauty is certainly more than skin-deep. As Janet Baker, the singer, wrote, about going to hear her colleague Lena Horne perform: 'We couldn't take our eyes off her, she has the charisma, the beauty, which comes from great discipline' (*Full Circle*, Penguin, 1984). Women have the potential to link physical and spiritual beauty. It is not easy; it requires struggle, choice and continual adjustment. The Queen of Beauty serves as a reminder that it can be done.

Images

Street Image

A beautiful, well-dressed woman; she pays great attention to make-up, grooming and clothes, but not in such a way as to stifle the personality underneath. She is on her way to the art gallery that she runs, where she will be presiding over a private viewing later in the day. There is a warmth and a radiance about her; her movements are measured, self-assured. People automatically look at her as she passes by. They think they have seen her somewhere before – was she on the television last night?

Mythic Image

Beauty queens of the past – Helen of Troy, Cleopatra; queens whose beauty silences opposition and inspires loyalty in their subjects. The Queen of Beauty appears in image; she may be glimpsed in a portrait, a miniature held in the hand of a knight or warrior as he rides off to battle; she may appear on film or television screen and be adored by millions. In her chamber, her naked sexuality is like a flickering tongue of flame playing over the body of her lover.

Personal Image

There are times when you sense that your body and soul are in harmony; you know that your outer image is a happy reflection of your inner state. Are you aware of your own beauty, or do you only glimpse it through the acknowledgement of others? What photographs of yourself give you pleasure? What is it about your image in them that you like? When you catch a glimpse of yourself in the mirror, what do you really see?

Evolution

Youth

In girlhood, there may be complete unselfconsciousness of beauty, although the child who is encouraged too young to consider her appearance becomes precocious and vain. In youth we struggle to match fashionable expectations against our own shadowy sense of self; it takes time for a secure identity to be born out of this. There are moments of natural awakening to one's own beauty, but it is rare that it is really appreciated in the early years of womanhood; usually it is taken for granted, and only lamented when it is gone.

Maturity

This is when the woman can make the very best of what she has, and what she is. She enjoys what she has; she may be less inhibited about experimenting with the outward image; on the other hand she is less of a slave to fashion, more ready to accept her individuality and express it openly. If her looks are appreciated, she takes it as a bonus, knowing that the passing of time makes such compliments precious.

Old Age

The challenge is to prevent habits such as greed, self-pity, and suspicion eating into the features and lines of the face. Maybe it is already too late. There is no hiding the character now by outward disguise. Beauty may still shine through, and is more moving in its way. Love, generosity and wisdom reveal themselves in visible beauty upon the wrinkled face of the old woman. There is rarely any real interest in fashion now, but it is heartening when some individuality of style and presence remains, and the frumpish 'old lady' image is avoided.

Manifestations

Gifts

Physical beauty. A sense of inner worth, and the talent for reflecting it in outer forms and appearances. An admirer who appreciates you; a lover who draws the best from you. Arts of colour and harmony; the ability to create beauty in the environment around you.

Trials

Loss of physical beauty. Mockery from others over one's appearance; withdrawal of external appreciation of your beauty. Situations of enforced anonymity; being compelled to wear uniforms, clothes chosen by others that offend your aesthetic sense. Growing old.

Rituals and Cults

Sessions at the make-up table, in dress shops, hairdressers and beauty parlours. Cults of fashion; cults of exclusive dress; the rigours bounding what is considered acceptable for the ball, the disco, the dinner party. Adornment with jewellery and gem stones. Beauty competitions. Rituals of bathing and tending the body. The cult of platonic love; the escalation of interaction between man and woman to a level above the sexual and the personal.

The Vision

Of divine beauty, reflected in the form and the presence of the feminine.

The Weaving Mother

Weaving

The craft of weaving requires threads that can be bound together, the skill to combine them, and knowledge of the patterns that can be formed. Those single threads can be woven into a new texture and shape that will bring out qualities not immediately apparent in the raw materials, such as intensity and shadings of colour, strength or delicacy of fabric. New forms are created that can contain, cover, connect or protect; the basket, the shawl, the rope and the tapestry are all examples of these. It needs vision to foresee what the finished product will look like, but it also needs skill, to set the process in motion and maintain it with economy of effort.

'Weaving' is thus taken in a broad sense here, and the Weaving Mother is a symbol for the process of choosing the raw material, making the threads, and binding them fast together. She is the organizing principle of the female, tying the bonds of love, weaving the pattern of daily life, and foreseeing the time when the last threads must be snipped. Through her craft, she turns simplicity into complexity, and complexity back to simplicity again. Each separate strand is simple, whether it is of cotton, cane or clay. The work in progress is complex, and can only proceed through use of method and skill, not by the eye alone. But the finished result has a unity and wholeness; there is cloth, for instance, where before there were only single silk threads; you can see how a pattern has emerged in the myriad tufts of wool, or a basket from unyielding spikes of cane. The Weaving Mother must know the beginning and the end of the process, or else the middle is just a meaningless jumble. You cannot pick up someone else's half-finished piece of knitting and carry on with no pattern to guide you.

The First Threads

I shall give some space in this chapter to considering the single threads, the first strands, how they are chosen and set into place. When this is understood, then the rest follows more easily. The most primitive of these first threads is the umbilical cord which binds mother to child. It is a strong, resilient, twisted rope to which the baby is attached in the womb, and through which it receives all nourishment until birth, when the cord is severed. Two lives are bound together by a cord, and if this were to be broken prematurely, one would die.

This basic fact of life has been recognized in teachings and in myths as intrinsic to the feminine psyche. In her autobiography, *Dancing in the Light*, the actress Shirley MacLaine mentions a school of Zen Buddhism founded in the fifteenth century by a Japanese master, Ikkyu. She relates:

He challenged Zen philosophy, which not only ignored but almost denied the existence of women and therefore the importance of love and sex between men and women in human life. He called his acceptance of human sexuality and respect for the female energy Red Thread Zen, acknowledging that life itself would not exist if not for the umbilical cord that connects us to the feminine.

(*Dancing in the Light*, Bantam Press, 1986)

Closer to Western culture is the ancient Greek myth of the three female Fates, Clotho, Lachesis and Atropos. One spun the thread of life, the second measured it and the third cut it. These actions corresponded to the formation of a new life, its allocation of good and evil influences, and its span of existence. Belief in these three Fates is said to have been very deep-rooted in Greece, and apparently survived in parts of the country almost till the present day, where birth customs included rites to propitiate these goddesses. Something of the sort may be apparent in the fairy tale of the Sleeping Beauty, where a curse is put upon the infant princess by the fairy left out of the christening party – a curse that is to come about, too, by means of a spinning wheel.

From a woman's body is formed the cord which binds the new life fast and brings it to birth in this world. It is probably the strongest human bond that we ever experience. The umbilical cord is the physical representation of the maternal bond, but of course there are other ways in which this bond operates. 'She who rocks the cradle rules the world' is a well-known saying. The emotional and mental link tying the child to its mother is usually very powerful, and goes on well after the physical birth itself. While the personality is forming, until the age of seven or eight or so, the child is closely identified with its mother, or whoever is the mother figure in the child's life. Little is done without reference to the mother, and the mother, for her part, may empathically share the child's feelings, and even know telepathically what the child is doing when out of sight. It is a symbiotic relationship, whose outward token was the umbilical cord, and which continues to be fed by the maternal bond until the two beings become separate.

It is likely that, at a deep level, some link remains between mother and child as long as both of them are alive. The twentieth-century psychologist, C. G. Jung, relates a dream he had the night before his mother's death:

I was in a dense, gloomy forest; fantastic, gigantic boulders lay about among huge jungle-like trees. It was a heroic, primeval landscape. Suddenly I heard a piercing whistle that seemed to resound through the whole universe. My knees shook. Then there were crashings in the underbrush, and a gigantic wolfhound with a fearful, gaping maw burst forth. At the sight of it, the blood froze in my veins. It tore past me, and I suddenly knew: the Wild Huntsman had commanded it to carry away a human soul. I awoke in deadly terror, and the next morning I received the news of my mother's passing.

(*Memories, Dreams, Reflections*, Collins, 1983)

Bonds

To form, use and sever cords is a feminine instinct that carries on throughout life, and not just in the process of physical motherhood. Some of these 'emotional bindings' go on at a level below the surface of normal awareness. Their power can be considerable, and knowledge of them is sometimes painful if attention is drawn to them. The ability of mother and child to form a bond with each other is not necessarily restricted to a blood relationship; it is an urge, a power, a need that may find other channels through which to operate, so that during our lives we may create more bonds of a similar nature, finding new 'mothers' or 'children' to attach ourselves to. Needless to say, such 'children' may be way beyond the age of infancy, and such 'mothers' no older than ourselves.

Similar to the process of forming maternal bonds, is that of forging sexual bonds. It is not always agreed whether it is the woman who first issues the invitation, or the male. Examine any relationship you have experienced; you may be confident that the initiative was taken by one party rather than the other, but was it? If there is no potential willingness in the woman to respond, then perhaps the man would never approach her. On the other hand, without some active energy from the man, what would she ever have found to be interested in? It is an intriguing issue.

Leaving aside the question of which came first, let us assume active interest on the part of the man, and a potential interest on the part of the woman. The next stage usually involves some resistance from the woman, and an escalation of the drive from the male to overcome this. (Just watch two pigeons on a roof engaged in their act of courtship.) The outcome is not yet certain. The woman can still choose to turn away completely, or if the male drive is not strong enough to break through the barriers, the couple may be mismatched and the interaction die away. (Remembering, of course, that there are instances where polarities can be reversed and a strong woman may prefer a man weaker than herself.)

Then comes a point, if matters continue, where the woman can suddenly experience her resistance crumbling, like a heavy door giving way before a battering ram pounding against it. She may be surprised, disconcerted; she may even have had no conscious intention of getting involved with this particular man. The way is open now; the channel is connected. Even though the relationship may be in its infancy, the current is set flowing and the Weaving Mother begins to spin her thread. The masculine energy is made available, and over a period of time the woman can crystallize that energy into a bond that will hold fast. It is like supplying a circuit for electricity, or turning a liquid into a solid. It is the same principle as the female body receiving the male sperm, and, after it has conjoined with the egg, nourishing it and gestating it so that its form can grow from fundamental simplicity to the complexity of a human body.

The bonds can be emotional, as well as physical, acting like invisible cords, conveying feeling, enthusiasms, energies, from one person to another. In the novel *Jane Eyre*, Mr Rochester, soon to be Jane's lover, says to her:

'I sometimes have a queer feeling with regard to you – especially when you are near me, as now: it is as if I had a string somewhere under my left ribs, tightly and inextricably knotted to a similar string situated in the corresponding quarter of your little frame. And if that boisterous Channel and two hundred miles or so of land come broad between us, I am afraid that cord of communion will be snapt; and then I've a nervous notion I should take to bleeding inwardly.'

(Charlotte Brontë, *Jane Eyre*, published in 1847. From Chapter 23)

Such bonds may build up before either party is fully aware of the connection, for they can be formed through a process of initiative and response at a very deep level. The process of bonding is related to the instinctive level of life; this instinctive level seeks to protect itself, and thus may often lie beyond the normal realms of consciousness. It would be highly dangerous if we had the choice of tampering with instinct. We do not have to 'choose' whether we breathe or whether our heart beats, for instance; it is better that the body carries on the process without interference. Certain psychological processes have something of this quality, too, and although we can achieve a degree of insight and control over them, they need to be handled with care. The drives that bind one person to another are primitive and intense, and can be disturbing to our normal perceptions if we allow ourselves to see what is going on.

I have been talking about experiences which affect both men and women; what I am suggesting is that the role of the Weaving Mother is to spin a thread, a bond, from the 'raw material' proffered by the male. If the woman does not choose to fulfil this part of the process, then the connection will not hold; by and large it is women who create the form of the relationship. However, looking at the archetype of the Weaving Mother operating in the general human domain, we can see the same principle operating in, for instance, the teaching systems of spiritual and esoteric traditions, where it may just as easily be the man who calls upon the powers of binding. This takes us out of the realm of male–female sexual relationships into another sphere, where such bonds can be used for better communication between individuals, and to foster the link between teacher and pupil. In any learning situation the teacher–pupil relationship can be a vulnerable and intense one, with some of the dependence of the mother–child interaction until the pupil is mature enough in that particular field of study to stand alone and make his or her own judgements. There is nothing intrinsically bad about such a link and it can be enormously helpful. But, of course, it can be abused, and serve as a means of adding to personal power, of drawing energy from others and manipulating them. Far from this happening only in the realm of serious study or occult practices, we come across numerous examples in daily life. There is person A, who seems to be strangely in the power of person B, and though he is deriving no visible benefit from the relationship, cannot break out of it. There are the lovers, where the apparently weaker one of the two seems to be the one calling the tune. There is the social acquaintance you do not feel comfortable being near, for it is as if she sucks something out of you and you come away feeling tired and dispirited.

We do have a choice as to whether to make the connection or

not, but, as I have said, unless one is aware of it forming at the time, the bond is likely to build up at the instinctive level. For instance, a woman may respond to the 'little boy' appeal of a man, and be caught by his 'need' of her. A seeker after spiritual truth may respond to the warmth of energy pouring from a guru, without ever questioning whether he wishes to become attached to the particular variety of truth represented. A man may show an interest in a woman, simply wanting to try out his style, and then find himself ensnared by the admiration and attention she beams at him. The more intellectual and sophisticated we become, the more we are tempted to assign all sorts of reasons to why we have contact with particular people. Favourite fairy tales are the need for spiritual growth, love at first sight, the pull of destiny or meetings in past lives, and we do not realize the primitive level of being in which the bond has its source.

The bonding process draws on the raw stuff of human emotions, sexual energy and the survival instinct. Used wisely, it can produce some truly remarkable relationships, and be the fuel which generates real love and knowledge. If it is left completely at the level of the unconscious, most of us will muddle through its manifestations. But to use it with inadequate or mistaken information is the most dangerous of all. The psychologist and the healer must be under rigorous discipline if they are not to fall into this trap. Vague idealism, and a general desire to help others are not enough in the way of protection, for other people too have power and drives which are seeking a focus. C. G. Jung was well aware of this, and in his book *The Psychology of the Transference* warns of the dangers that lurk when the mind of the psychologist opens to that of the patient. He points out that he has come across cases where, a link having been formed between the two, the patient has had phases of extraordinary well-being and health during which his psychologist has succumbed to severe mental malaise.

Spinning, Measuring and Cutting the Thread

The association of the mother and the umbilical cord with the spider, who spins a thread out of her own body, has not passed unnoticed. A Greek myth tells us that Arachne, a young woman living in Lydia, was famous for her skills in spinning and weaving. She was reckless enough to challenge the goddess Athene, patroness of those crafts, to a contest of skill. Alas, mythology usually relates that those who dare to challenge the gods pay a stiff price for their temerity. Arachne's contribution was a woven hanging on which she had depicted the lives and loves of the gods. When Athene came to inspect the work she could find no flaw there. Furious at such perfection, she turned Arachne into a spider, condemning her to spin thread from her own body and to be weaving a web for ever after. What is the moral of this story? Perhaps that we can be too clever for our own good; those who spin and weave the complexities of human relationships are likely to get caught in their own tangles one day. Or perhaps it is that if we try to take on the identity and authority of the Weaving Mother the consequences will be severe; our own personal weavings are only part of a much greater pattern, which we cannot control or take credit for. We can use the skills and potential revealed to us by each archetype, but should recognize that they emanate from a source beyond our individual powers. Or perhaps it is that life is simply not fair, and that skill and cunning are what we should be using to navigate its choppy waters, rather than making open displays of bravado against the odds.

So far I have covered the spinning of the thread – and something of 'measuring its length', the job of the second Fate, Lachesis. For women, the measurement of the thread has to do with continuity; it is the thread that runs through all complexity, an underlying order linking past and future. Women like to know the sequence of events. The chronology of the past is important, and we feel easier in our minds if our memories are ordered, even if this only means remembering whether the gas man came on Thursday or Friday. In the household, we may find ourselves acting as 'memory' to the whole family, both in the prosaic sense of keeping lists of jobs and obligations in mind, and also in the sense of building up an extended record of family life with photos, souvenirs and diaries.

It also seems to be more of a woman's forte to keep in touch with what is happening in the future. Most men of my acquaintance revel in happy ignorance when it comes to knowing plans and dates for the weeks ahead. Women want to feel the thread that runs into the future. It is an area where a woman may gain control over a man, for while he gaily assumes that the present is spontaneous, and the future an open book, she is quietly mapping out the course of future events and by the time he wakes up to this fact it is too late to do much about it.

Again, this aspect of the female psyche may have some relation to the basic mother–child connection. A young child has to have continuity in its life, and the mother has to help create this. The child cannot make sense of the world without pattern, without events that repeat. If a child is told that a particular outing is to take place tomorrow, this becomes a certain fact in his or her mind. Literature and autobiography are liberally sprinkled with accounts of the indignation and outrage felt when such a promise fails to materialize. Indeed, I think that Virginia Woolf's novel *To the Lighthouse* is largely based around this theme. The thread of continuity is also a gift that a woman can give to a man. Theseus would still be blundering around in the labyrinth where he went to slay the Minotaur, if Ariadne had not given him a ball of thread so that he could retrace his steps when the deed was done.

Cutting the threads is a great test. Atropos, with her shears, was feared more than the other two Fates. Hers is the gesture of finality. To perform it, one must know when the thread is long enough, or when the cloth being woven is complete. It requires detachment. In the West, we women usually give over the responsibility of cutting the umbilical cord to the midwife or doctor, and I think it would require considerable courage and will to do this ourselves. We rely on others to make that crucial separation for us, between the two bodies that have been physically linked all through the gestation period. Would it perhaps affect our outlook on the mother–child relationship if we had to take this responsibility on ourselves? We tend to assume that significant rituals are only found in 'primitive' societies and in state ceremonies such as the Coronation. In fact there are many acts woven into the fabric of our everyday lives which have just such an importance, which may critically influence our relationships with others. It is part of the art of mothering to be able to let go, when the time comes; we have all met sturdy adults who are 'tied to mother's apron strings', often in many subtle, insidious little ways. Releasing the emotional threads is somewhat like cutting the umbilical cord: if it is done too soon, both parties risk severe injury through loss of blood, whereas if it is left too long, it becomes an obscenity, a viscous, unnatural-looking projection of the human body. It is usual for the placenta (the afterbirth) and the cord to be burnt, and in many countries there are purifying ceremonies surrounding birth, signifying the cleansing and separating of one body from another. The first physical separation must later be followed by a psychological separation so that the child can become an independent adult.

For a woman, letting go may be one of the hardest things she has to do. Men may suffer just as much when a relationship fails, but they seem able to make a cleaner break. A woman may convince herself that if she holds on, is patient, and tries to change things, she can bring it back to life. Any small hope held out to her by circumstances, or by her lover, is as a wisp which she can spin and twist into a thread, and if she gathers enough of these her feelings tell her that she will be able to bind them into a strong rope. Occasionally, of course, this does work, but it carries the risk of an even more painful separation later if the pledge is not renewed gladly and willingly on both sides. There are many variations on this theme; there are, for instance, the men who feel imprisoned by a bond, but, who, when it is broken, panic and want to build it up again, so creating a cycle which can run and run until one partner changes in attitude. But a woman *can* say: 'No more,' and cut the thread. She may even find, if a relationship has been a particularly draining one, that this brings sweet relief and restores her zest for life.

This may be a lengthy discourse on the 'single thread', but it is important to investigate these basics, for when they are known, the multiple interactions, the complexities of the weaving process itself, become far easier to understand. In describing each of the nine archetypes, it is my aim to uncover the forces

45

which lie at the heart of their 'beings'. It would be unsatisfying just to look at the ultimate refinement of their natures; the picture becomes too perfect and stylized. Myths themselves are full of contradictions and inconsistencies. Very often, when they sound pallid and over-precise, the versions we have received are their latest re-telling, too smooth and polished, fixed and logical. Often, by digging a little deeper into their history, we can uncover far more interesting antecedents, cracks and all, which in their rough-hewn shape stimulate a more vital response.

Skills and Interaction

The threads that a woman holds she weaves into the fabric of daily life. Creating this pattern may be so much second nature to her, that she does not recognize the skill involved and the complexity of her art. A senior executive of a business once told me that he had difficulty in getting women employees to realize and make known such skills in the working environment. Many, he said, were convinced that they had had no managerial experience, yet they had successfully brought up children, run a home, and far more. Part of his role was to encourage them to define these skills then present them as qualifications, and transfer them into the business context.

Rearing a child is a formative process, requiring diverse skills and a sense of how the pattern is taking shape, and the extent to which it must grow before it is complete. There are skills of every kind to be learned, from changing a nappy to knowing whether or not to call the doctor, when to teach the facts of life, and how to develop the parent–child relationship during adolescence. We learn such skills from our mothers, midwives, books and from our own inner promptings, and as we use them they become absorbed into everyday life, often so much so that we no longer realize just how much we have learnt and are capable of; in fact, we only take notice of the areas in which we feel that we fail. It is a common problem for a woman to undervalue herself, being aware only of what she cannot, rather than what she can, do. The business executive was right. Many of the skills we acquire on the most mundane level are exactly the same as those that are needed in any high-powered job – the ability to manage people, to organize schedules, make the most of limited resources, to keep calm in a crisis, and to encourage those dependent upon us. Ideally, we should not need others to point this out to us, but be alert to our own capabilities and ready to use them in another context.

Weaving creates new qualities by combining separate elements; different colours and textures emerge as the patterns are formed. Taking an example from the social level, one can have a great deal of fun, and even work a bit of mischief, through planning and giving a small-scale party. Too large a party, and groups of guests who know each other can split off on their own. But with, say, twelve to twenty people, a highly interesting combination can be selected and by a little judicious manoeuvring the different elements set to interact. Consider such an occasion: suppose that each person has arrived entirely on his or her own, knowing only the hostess. By the end of the evening, a multitude of cross-connections will have been formed. First of all, the guests will search for existing connections, such as people and places they know in common, or films they have seen, and establish a network that way. They will exchange opinions, becoming united in their views or strongly opposed to each other. They will share hopes, problems, enthusiasms, trade knowledge, offer advice, relate their plans. Some may make arrangements to meet again. By the end of the evening an extraordinarily complex pattern will have been woven, initiated by just one person.

Again, this is not only a woman's prerogative. But women tend to work by manipulating the threads, setting up a pattern to be woven, which may not be fully revealed until much later. The male objective – so I am told – when entering a new group of people, is to work out its power structure. This may involve challenge and competition, finding out who is the apparent top dog and who the underdog. Women, on the whole, would rather keep the shuttle moving, the threads intertwining, watching the patterns of response form. The classic example of this is the girl who sets two men fighting for her. She sits and watches, and they do not even realize that she has provoked them to it. The heroine of Bizet's opera *Carmen* is a prime case, passionate in love but also calculating, provocative and infuriating as she teases and ensnares men, bringing out the most dangerous and violent side of their natures. Until tragedy and fate catch up with her she is always mistress of the situation, coolly self-possessed. I think many women would like just a touch of the Carmen quality in their lives.

The detachment of the weaver was remarked on earlier. The artist may live passionately through every brush-stroke, but the weaver cannot – she needs a clear head and a sense of the goal before her if she is to make order and substance out of the strands with which she works. Sometimes she works mechanically, and this can be disturbing. One is reminded of the story of French women calmly knitting at the guillotine, while heads rolled. In lighter vein, something of the sort is captured by the wry humour of 'The Knotting Song':

> Hears not my Phillis how the birds
> Their feather'd mates salute?
> They tell their passion in their words,
> Must I alone, must I alone be mute?
> Phillis without a frown or smile
> Sat and knotted, and knotted and knotted
> and knotted all the while.

> The god of love in thy bright eyes
> Does like a tyrant reign;
> But in thy heart a child he lies
> Without his dart, without his dart or flame.
> Phillis without a frown or smile
> Sat and knotted, and knotted and knotted
> and knotted all the while.

> So many months in silence past,
> And yet in raging love,
> Might well deserve one word at last
> My passion, my passion should approve.
> Phillis without a frown or smile
> Sat and knotted, and knotted and knotted
> and knotted all the while.

48

Must then your faithful swain expire,
And not one look obtain,
Which he to soothe his bond desire,
Might pleasingly, might pleasingly explain?
Phillis without a frown or smile,
Sat and knotted, and knotted and knotted,
and knotted all the while.
(Words by Sir Charles Sedley; set to music by Henry Purcell)

I can imagine the rise in colour and temperature of the 'faithful swain' when meeting such a display of cool indifference. I can imagine, too, the ladies of Jane Austen's era resorting to their needles and knotting, in order to retain a serene calm in the face of male blustering and boasting.

The plotting which accompanies the skill of weaving is actually carried out in advance. That is, the scheming as to choice of materials, designs and technique is all done ahead of the process itself. At the emotional level, this can mean that the personal involvement is engaged ahead of the action, and that by the time the manipulation is actually taking effect, its originator can sit back and observe what she has set in motion. This is why skilled manipulators are so hard to catch 'on the job'. Groups of teenage girls are expert at the procedure. By the time they walk down the street, just happening to bump into the gang of boys, they have got it all worked out. They may giggle and act as though they have not a serious thought in their heads, but they know exactly what they are up to. They know which boy each of them has her eye on, and if there is any clash of interest, they will deal with it in advance, too. They know where they want to go, and what they are willing to do. Any previous encounters will have been picked over a dozen times, the characters of the boys analysed in tedious detail, and interesting future possibilities considered. The boys, on the other hand, are concerned about looking big in each other's estimation, and they are usually innocent of all except the most rudimentary manoeuvring tactics. The girls, by comparison, are as organized as a professional team of jewel thieves.

The webs which are woven are many and varied. There are plenty of physical weavings: there are tapestries, rugs, knitted clothes, cat's cradles, plaits, maypole ribbons; there is knotting, crochet, basket-weaving, pot-coiling and many more skills which are all of the same basic craft. The Weaving Mother is not her products, though. She knows that they come to life under her touch, and that they may carry their own life and their creator be forgotten. No one knows now who made those fine antique rugs that you see in the museum. No one is quite certain who invented Fair Isle knitting patterns, or the steps of the maypole dance where ribbons are woven round each other. The mother who lives only through her children will face an empty future, for she is losing touch with the source of her own life, identifying with her creations and expecting them to sustain her. The promise of the Weaving Mother is that you may cast off your threads when the pattern is complete, and begin again. There are always new threads that can be spun, new colours to work with, new shapes to fashion.

Images

Street Image

She's busy and alert, writing in her notebook, or studying a street map. Her hair is cut into a neat, glossy skull-cap and her clothes are smart and spare in style. She's very much aware of what is going on around her, even though she's working on her latest project. When she has finished what she is doing for the moment, she walks on briskly, her head making little bird-like movements, so that she can see everything that she passes.

Mythic Image

The helpful thread of Ariadne; the artistic weavings of Arachne; the spinning and snipping of the three Fates. The skilful Weaving Mother, ready to teach her craft to others; the frightening one, holding the threads of your life; the jealous one, owner of the web and namer of its patterns. Her sounds are the whirring of the spinning wheel, the rhythmic clacking of the loom, and the cold, metallic clipping of the shears.

Personal Image

What is your craft? What skills have you learnt that you can apply deftly, and cleverly? There is a certainty in your touch when you use them: know and be proud of them, discover further uses for them. What are the threads that make up the pattern of your life? See the deepest bonds and drives of all, and then, weaving over and around them, the light and shade of work and leisure, love, ambition and desire. Gently behold and test the web of your life; see whether it responds to your touch.

Evolution

Youth

In childhood, she's a girl with endless half-finished projects strewn around her room. She wants to try out everything – sculpting, knitting, clay-modelling, sketching – you name it. How to look through a microscope, operate the computer, propagate plants. In adolescence she's mischievous; what's the point of having brains and beauty if you can't have some fun with them?

Maturity

The organized woman, weaving as many threads into her pattern as she possibly can. She has to decide, as she goes, how and when to weave in new strands and drop old ones, still keeping the continuity of design. There is temptation to prove herself, by handling conflicting, stressful elements, by taking on too much, but at this stage the wisdom of discrimination usually shows itself. Acquired expertise and skill give her the confidence to make the choices that will shape her future.

Old Age

Active engagement may give way to the skills of contemplation and reflection. Think of Miss Marple, Agatha Christie's aged detective heroine, knitting her unceasing supply of pink and blue baby garments, pondering the latest murder case and quietly arriving at the solution long before anybody else. The hands may be kept busy so that the mind can reflect, and see the pattern inherent in the tangled mass of threads.

Manifestations

Gifts

Physical and mental dexterity; finely tuned perceptions. The ability to handle several activities at once. Humour at the absurdity of events. An eye for the significant among the trivial. Skills in human relationships.

Trials

Loss of skill through illness or accident. Loss of control over events. The dulling of the senses with age. Becoming entangled in the web you have woven; after all, 'it seemed like a good idea at the time'. Accusations from others of being nosey, bossy, overmanaging.

Rituals and Cults

The education of girls and young women – intellectual, emotional and sexual. Skills that are passed on from mother to daughter. Craft work; women's crafts as they are designated in different times and places, such as midwifery, sewing, cooking, undertaking, writing. Aspects of divination, such as the drawing up of a horoscope. Sessions of gossip, plotting and intrigue with other women.

The Vision

Of order in the universe; of our ability to take the raw materials and weave them into a pattern of our choosing.

3

The Lady of Light

It was a beautiful summer's night. I was staying on a large country estate, taking part in a week's music course. Leaving the main building at bedtime, I walked back through the old walled garden, the churchyard, and down the grassy lane to the cottage annexe where I had my room. To my delight, dotted here and there on the leafy verge were gleams of light, a pale luminous shining in the warm darkness. They were glow-worms, the first I had ever seen. Later in the week, some of us went for an evening swim at a nearby beach – or rather not so nearby, as it entailed a few miles of driving and then a long walk down a deserted track. By the time we arrived at the sea, those of us who did not know that stretch of coastline were completely removed from any sense of place or direction. It was just us, on a long stretch of sand, with the dark sea ahead of us – a landscape which might go on into infinity, as far as we could tell. It was a starry night, and as we swam there was light in the water, sparkling, rippling, starlight playing on our fingers and the smooth seal-like lines of our bodies.

Both experiences summed up, for me, a rare quality of joy, a close approach to perfection that this particular week embodied. Such times are unusual, yet they do occur; with hindsight, they often seem to have been the result of the right combination of people, time and place. They cannot be predicted, or deliberately devised. Indeed, as expectations can kill the magic stone dead, such occasions are often evoked by going somewhere completely new. Starlight and glow-worm light captured for me the simplicity of this joy. It did not have to be on a vast scale, dazzling or absolute. It was an in-dwelling quality – the light of the tiny glow-worm, the light dancing in the waves.

Light is such an absolute, yet such a commonplace, that it is difficult to know where to start when discussing it. We take it for granted that we have light to see by, natural or artificial. At the other extreme, light can be thought of as the final and complete revelation of spiritual reality. In considering any symbol which has light as an essential quality, we are open to a bewilderingly large span of concepts, both physical and metaphysical. To find some meaning for the Lady of Light, a feminine version of light and an equal member of a set of nine archetypes, I think it is necessary to veer away from speculations about the ultimate nature of light, and look instead at specific qualities that she may embody. In my own experience, a dozen glow-worms were enough to kindle a sense of delight, and to establish a lasting image in my mind as a distillation of that week's happiness. I did not need a vast beacon lit on a hilltop.

The Lady of Light may appear in our lives in three different ways, expressing a relationship between the feminine and light. She is there at a general, collective level; she may also reveal herself as a polarized force; and again as the inner light of the individual. All these can be known in quite specific manifestations and not just as abstract truths. I shall give pointers to these, which readers' own experience and understanding can fill out.

The Collective Light

It seems that there is a difference between the light of the masculine and the light of the feminine, in their natural, fundamental expressions. The feminine light is in-dwelling, suffused, and radiates out. The masculine is beamed, intense and focused. In broad psychological terms, it can be said that the male is achievement-orientated, directing his efforts towards a specific goal, whereas the woman is more concerned that the differing elements in her life should be in harmonious relation to one another, and that the circle of light in which she is centred includes them all.

This quality of inclusion signifies the sense of the collective that women have, and from which they can draw strength in their lives. A light that radiates out from its source can dissolve personal limits, blending with other such pools of light to form a greater circle. Over the last couple of decades, feminists have been rediscovering the pleasures of 'sisterhood'. With cries of joy, it has been announced that women need not depend upon men for companionship and understanding; women's groups have become a commonplace, and support and friendship between women re-evaluated. It is certainly true that women meeting and working together can find a sustaining, natural pleasure in their interaction. I noticed it especially on one occasion when I was beset with problems which had made me very unhappy. I was due to attend a meeting with several other women whom I knew and felt in sympathy with, and when I arrived there, the weight of my unhappiness just rolled off me like an unwanted burden. I didn't even need to think about my personal difficulties again at that time. The company of the other women created a medium in which we felt happy and fulfilled, a medium that was almost tangible, like water or air. Perhaps in societies where women in the extended family or tribe naturally spend a lot of time together, there is a healthier, more relaxed attitude to life.

But was sisterhood ever really lost, as some may claim? I am doubtful; I suggest that we have all just become more aware of it in recent years, more ready to take it into new forms. Many girls at school derive enormous strength from their peer groups; women in previous generations had their own societies and formed strong bonds with neighbours and friends. In my case, growing up just before the new wave of feminism, I consider that the transition from adolescence to adulthood was effected by participation in a strong peer group of girls at school. We were all highly individualistic – in fact, what we had in common seemed to be a reputation for rebellion and trouble-making – but we shared a way into adult life, influencing each other and creating a collective strength. Our discussions ranged through the whole spectrum of life, from the sublime to the trivial, and while I do not now remember many of the conclusions that we reached then, the quality of that communication is still with me.

We entered each other's lives, and knew each other in essence.

In some respects, today's emphasis on women's rights, literature and issues may not only be a drive to increase women's standing in relation to men, but may rather be a celebration of the rediscovery of the shared communication that women have. It has always been there – from the suffragettes to the Women's Institute – but many of the older forms have become outmoded and new ones are needed which are relevant to the modern age. There is even a physical basis to the collectivity of women: it has been shown that women living together over a length of time frequently fall into a synchronicity of menstrual cycles. (See Penelope Shuttle and Peter Redgrove, *The Wise Wound – Menstruation and Everywoman.*)

The collectivizing force of women is a strong one, and not without its problems. Although structures of hierarchy and authority can be used by women, the natural feminine tendency is towards cooperation, unification and agreement. Women can form a communal bond quickly, but may be reluctant to stand up for their personal views. At its worst, this can result in a lack of morality. More often, it turns into loss of direction or of purposeful organization, because no one is willing to separate herself from the rest in order to take charge.

I was once invited to a weekend conference of 'rural women' to give a workshop on astrology. It was a dismal, disorganized weekend and a waste of valuable opportunity; everything was left to 'flow', which in practice meant that many events did not even get off the ground. Time-keeping was out of the question, structure was notable largely by its absence, and at the end of the weekend someone stole the funds, thus breaking even the bond of collective trust which was assumed to exist. The only organized contingent were the men, who had been relegated to run the crèche in a nearby hall, set up each morning with military precision. However, it seemed that each sex could have learnt something from the other on this occasion; by the end of the day, the beautifully laid-out nursery, ready to provide the young arrivals with constructive play activities, was reduced to utter chaos from the tidal force of juvenile anarchy.

When I suggest that women have a strong ability to communicate with each other and form a collective body, it is not to imply that the individual should lose herself entirely in this. A pool of light is formed from several smaller pools of personal light, but the source of each single light must be acknowledged too. Because it is so easy for women to slip into a shared area with each other, they may at times have a fear of doing so, in case they lose their individuality. For a man, this does not seem to be so much of a problem; he can be one of a squadron of marching, identically dressed soldiers, or one of a thousand employees in a firm, and still *know* that he is special and unique. Women may fear the loss of their identity much more, because they know how easily they can merge with others. Young women may be reluctant to join long-established organizations which are patronized chiefly by older women, because they fear it will somehow drown their own up-to-date and dynamic image. Older women may hesitate to join in with the young, feeling that they may have to ape their manners to be accepted by them. Sometimes women need to make an effort to stretch the circle wider, and a newcomer will have to enter it, knowing that she does not fit in easily, but that her presence may transform it.

Women's collectivity can be used as a basis of cooperation, for sharing tasks, or giving mutual support. The basic association of men is not cooperative, but directional. It may show itself in the formation of groups with a hierarchical power structure, or as an outwardly driving force, such as is found in a hunting group. Women can certainly be competitive as individuals, but are less so at the group level; many of us who went to all-girls' schools found the competitive team sports at worst a real trial and at best something of a joke, even though we were quite prepared to put ourselves out in an individual context. Too much had been taken from the ethos of the boys' schools, including blazers and ties, which are hangovers from male attire of the Edwardian era. Our more natural inclination was to hide in the dim recesses of the games shed and carry on enthralling discussions about boyfriends and the origins of the universe.

A group of women can take in another who is thoroughly

miserable, and if she allows herself to join in, she can find herself much restored by the general strength there. Just being with other women and doing practical, even frivolous things, can be enormously helpful. It can restore an innocent pleasure in life at times of weariness and emptiness. It can dissolve boundaries of age and culture, and is, in effect, a way of bringing back faith. At this point a woman may be glad to be released, temporarily, from the struggle with her individual problems, and to be renewed by the light that her sisters generate.

When women find they are divided, they will seek to rejoin each other across that division. Expectant mothers, for instance, treated in isolation by doctors and hospitals, and without their own female relatives around to help them, flock to childbirth classes where often strong social contacts are made, which may last throughout the period of coping with a young baby and longer. We have fought long and hard for a certain amount of privacy in society, especially within the home, but this has not been without cost, and now we search for ways of re-establishing the collective level, as it is a part of women's nature to do.

Polarization: The 'Other'

We have looked at the idea of a female, in-dwelling, general light, which radiates out even though we may scarcely be aware of it. As our awareness of this quality of light increases, we may perceive it as centring on another figure – an inner or outer 'Lady of Light' – or as an identifiable principle to which we can begin to relate. The third stage, described later in this chapter, is to become that light principle consciously, and to work with it.

The Lady of Light can be seen as a 'guiding light'. Women may find her image within themselves, or see her reflected in a mythical, historical or living person who carries such a quality in her being. Guide, teacher and saint can all be representatives of the 'Lady of Light'. The need for guidance is not, of course, restricted to the female sex, and it could be very tricky trying to distinguish the essential differences between male and female archetypes of the guide. However, I think it can be looked at in another, much simpler way. Women need a guiding female principle to relate to, and this becomes representative of their own aspirations, ideals and future. This is not the mother, who lays down a ground plan for life and provides nourishment; she is not of the future. And it is not masculine, because whatever male teachers and guides a woman has, she still needs the inspirational feminine which resonates with her own being.

Many women will remember with gratitude one or two female teachers, who lit the way forward. We do not remember them for all the facts which they rammed into our heads, nor for praise or punishment, but for the way that they seemed to recognize our inner selves, and spoke to our essence. They were able to communicate with the part of us that longs to grow and expand into the world. If such an experience can be recalled, it usually has the quality of being a person-to-person contact, not necessarily as equals in understanding, but cutting right through the barriers of status and age.

A woman teacher can become a role model for female students, in a way that a male one does not. Having had both male and female teachers, in various adult contexts, I am intrigued by the differences. A male teacher can antagonize you, attract you, provoke you into working harder, and make you aware of aspects of yourself that you did not know existed; if these have potential, a man can apply a useful sort of pressure to make you develop them. But a woman teacher can know you from the inside; you cannot hide from her so easily, or divert her attention. She will recognize your being, and it may seem as if the light she is shining is a cold one at times. In a working relationship between female teacher and pupil there can be a healthy realism.

In the form of a mythical or historical figure, the Lady of Light can become more idealized. Perhaps the most obvious example is the fairy godmother, who appears, through popular expectation, in most pantomimes and a great many fairy stories. Just when circumstances are their darkest, the fairy godmother appears in a wonderful burst of light, waves her magic wand, and grants the heroine's dearest wishes. We know that there is someone, somewhere, who can make everything bloom again; this is the Lady of Light, the fairy godmother who might turn up one day if we are lucky.

Women such as Florence Nightingale, and Mother Theresa in our own day, are symbols of a very real struggle to light the way through darkness. Both have contended with disease and suffering, and have been seen as near-saints by a grateful and admiring public. The light-bearing principle which they represent (in Florence Nightingale's case, she was known as 'The Lady with the Lamp') can remain in the public imagination long after the personality has been forgotten. Florence Nightingale has been the inspiration for twentieth-century nursing; every now and then a historian attempts to point out that there may have been aspects of her life which were not quite so saintly as we believe, but this does not shatter her image. Once a person has attained archetypal status in the eyes of the world, it is very hard to break it.

The 'Lady of Light' may be experienced as an internal source. Either through work which involves training the imagination (in the sense of being an 'image-making' faculty) or spontaneously, a woman may have an intimation of a female guide, a feminine presence that watches over her life. She, the guide, may seem to be several steps removed from the hurly-burly of normal life, living in another dimension, having a clearer vision of past and future than we normally attain. Her presence may not always be directly accessible, and may be felt more strongly in times of crisis. The forms may vary. To be very specific is dangerous, because if we attempt to clothe the image too precisely it becomes restricted, less of 'light' and more of 'substance', and the life may go from it. One night, when I was going through a particularly troubled time, I awoke from restless, turbulent dreams, and, half-waking, had the sense of a woman sitting by my bed, watching over me. If I had to describe her, I would say that she was a sensible, down-to-earth woman, dressed plainly and cleanly, understanding what I was experiencing, yet sighing at my folly and patiently keeping an eye on me till I was in a stronger state again. I do not expect to encounter 'the Lady' in that particular form again; she represented a power to watch over and sustain me, and her qualities were ones that were especially lacking in my own life at that time – practicality, solidity and a refusal to get flustered. Images are a wonderful means of giving us insight, but they should not be pinned down too firmly. An archetype can appear in many different ways, each an interpretation of that central principle, with its own particular significance.

Knowing that we have access to a source of light, we can learn to use it. The ways of using feminine light are beautifully described by Robert A. Johnson in his book, *She – Understanding Feminine Psychology*. Appropriately enough for this stage of development, where the light is identified as a separate source, he equates it with the lamp in the myth of Psyche and Eros. Psyche, so lovely that she cannot find a mortal husband, is condemned to be the bride of Death. She is rescued from this fate however by Eros, the god of Love, who himself falls in love with her. He takes her to live in the Valley of Paradise, where all her desires are met except one, which is to see the face of her husband. She is told that if she catches sight of him when he visits her in the darkness, he will leave her. Spurred on by her envious sisters, who convince her that her mystery spouse is really a foul serpent, she arms herself with a lamp to see him with and knife to attack him with. When she sees, to her astonishment, by the light of the lamp, that her mate is the god of Love, she does not attack him, but it is too late to stop him from flying away. The rest of the myth concerns Psyche's trials until she is eventually reunited with Eros on Mount Olympus.

Johnson equates Psyche's lamp with the female ability to shine a light on aspects of life which are in darkness to the male. He maintains that women are granted the power to illuminate, and that they can use this wisely, even though men may be reluctant to face up to what is revealed:

A man depends largely on the woman for the light in the family, as he is often not very good at finding meaning for himself ... With a few words a woman can give meaning to a whole day's struggle, and a man will be very grateful. A man knows and wants this; he will edge up to it; he will initiate little occasions so that a woman can shed light for him ... This is part of the light-bearing quality of a woman.

The touch of light ... is a fiery thing. It often stings a man into awareness, which is partly why he fears the feminine so much. A woman, or his anima, often leads a man into new consciousness. It is almost always the woman who says, 'Let's sit down and talk about where we are.' A man does not often say this. The woman is the carrier of evolution for him in one way or another. She sometimes lights him into a new kind of relationship. The man is terrified of that, but he is equally terrified at the loss of it. Actually, a man greatly appreciates a woman who bears a lamp; he depends on the feminine light more deeply than most men are willing to admit.

Johnson also makes the point that, in terms of the myth, the light of the lamp reveals a god, and that this is also true in the human psychological context:

When Psyche lighted the lamp, she expected to see a beast, but she saw a god. To women, man is often either a god or a beast. When I have the courage, I can say that when one truly shows the light upon another person, he finds a god or goddess ... The same is true when a woman is finally able consciously to see her animus, her inner Eros. She finds that it is godlike.

(Robert A. Johnson, *She – Understanding Feminine Psychology*)

Working with the Light

If we make use of the light principle within ourselves, this can affect our own lives and those of others. In its freest operation it is a medium for inspiration and creativity. The diffused light, which we started with at the collective level, has become a powerful current, and we ourselves can be the channel for it. A close analogy with the art of singing can be made here. When a woman's voice is used freely and has power, it can sound and feel like a flow of light. Studying voice production does not mean that a voice is artificially manufactured, but that the body is trained so that the voice may be 'uncovered'. The body is taught to be a well-disciplined, physically strong, yet immensely sensitive organism, into which breath is taken and from which breath is released as sound. At its best, singing can feel like a river of light flowing through a firm yet flexible channel. When the basic flow is established, the light can be allowed to sparkle, dance, or be steady, glowing, smooth or rippling, according to the music that is being expressed. Singing is one of those activities which seems perfectly simple and natural when it is working well, but which requires, for most of us, years of discipline and effort to perfect. And even when the body is capable of such response, slight variations in external conditions and our own changing state may throw the process out of alignment. Constant work is needed, not just through physical efforts, but by using mental and emotional powers too, to recreate this balance which enables the voice to be released in an effortless stream of sound.

I have suggested that singing is a good analogy for the discovery and use of the light principle; I would go one step further and say that it is a literal example of this process. In this, it corresponds to other artistic modes. Working in dance, painting, writing or theatre can all have the effect, through training, effort and love of the art, of releasing in a woman her source of creative light. This may come more naturally and easily to some than to others, but it is possible that where a prolonged conscious effort has been made to tap this creative source, greater understanding and appreciation result than where only little work has been needed.

Stepping gingerly on to more dangerous ground, I would also suggest that women are more able to give direct expression to the light principle through creative and artistic activity than through religious involvement. I am talking here about organized religion, and structured religious forms seem to be based on predominantly 'light' or 'dark' principles. Religions which are 'light-based' usually exalt the masculine force more strongly than the feminine, and female followers of such religions have to approach the central mystery through the masculine pole. Christianity is such a religion: God is worshipped through Christ, the male principle, and the affirmation of light is found nowhere more clearly than in the opening chapter of St John's gospel, which includes the verses :

And the light shineth in darkness; and the darkness comprehended it not.

There was a man sent from God, whose name was John.

The same came for a witness, to bear witness of the Light, that all men through him might believe.

He was not that Light, but was sent to bear witness of that Light.

That was the true Light, which lighteth every man that cometh into the world.

(John, Chapter I, verses 5–9)

The religious way which has the feminine at its heart is that of entering deep darkness to find the mysteries of the divine. I do not think any of today's major religions have this as their central theme, although it may be found in religions of the past, and in various modern cults and sects. Of course, all religions have elements of both male and female within them; Christianity has the Virgin Mary, and its mystics have described the 'deep and dazzling darkness' which they must enter to know God. However, in any particular religion or sect, one of these principles, the light or the dark, is chosen above the other. The embodiment of light is masculine, that of the dark is feminine, and thus a religion based on the former will tend to be served by priests, and one based on the latter by priestesses.

What does it mean to be a priestess? We have female priests today, but no priestesses, except in the magical tradition. Why is the word regarded with some revulsion among the orthodox religions? Rather than only training women to take on roles that have been shaped by men over the centuries, would it not be far more interesting, more expansive, to look into the questions of priestesshood, to find out what mystery it is that women can touch on, and how they can communicate it to the human world? Perhaps there are clues in the archetype of the Great Mother; we must bear in mind, though, that we cannot go back to some primitive image of the priestess, but must give it life and meaning in today's terms. Tradition serves as a guide, not an absolute.

Although we are now talking mainly about darkness, rather than light, this is not entirely irrelevant to the Lady of Light. Her instinctive creativity, and her association with the future rather than the past, could be the fuel which helps us to generate new forms and roles for women today. Of all the nine, her form is perhaps the least defined, and her inspiration spread the most widely.

Perhaps the tremendous upsurge of female creativity over the last hundred years or so, particularly in the fields of literature and art, may be connected with the increasing desire of women to use for themselves 'the light principle'. They have found that the structure of existing religion does not, on the whole, provide a direct channel for expression and turn to individual creations instead.

Another way of clarifying the difference between the creative and the religious, in this context, might be to use those well-worn terms, 'active' and 'passive'. Let us suppose that male and female each have an active and a passive means of expressing light. The naturally 'active' light of the female is the generalized, collective light described at the beginning of the chapter. It affirms her unity with other women, and with the world, and is an active expression of integration. Without dwelling too long on the masculine side, the natural tendency of the male to 'beam out' light is actually a passive one; he does it without thinking. But at the level we have now reached, the male is the active principle, embodying creative, spiritual light, and can be its representative, as a saviour or as a priest. For a woman, releasing the creative process in herself is in fact a passive state. She has to work tremendously hard, but this is like building the banks of the river for it to flow through. When she has created the right conditions, the light comes through from a source beyond her vision, with its own energy and life. She can tap that source, channel the current, and direct it outwardly, but she herself is not that source; she is a container for it.

Women may have the advantage of being less fixed in the way they can express the creative light. I have suggested that the channels for the light can be made strong through effort, training and discipline; this is mainly for a particular purpose, such as writing or singing. But if the being of an individual woman is sufficiently strong and well-developed, then, knowing that light to be there deep within her, she can allow it to permeate the whole of her presence, refining and changing her very substance rather as a lamp when it is lit makes an apparently opaque glass shade appear translucent. This 'allowing' of the light to shine through seems to bring us back, full circle – a most appropriate feminine symbol – to the collective again. If women are capable of releasing the creative light within themselves, then it will be disseminated among the collective, but in a more potent way, with greater possibilities for transformation. A group of women who have all, as individuals, reached this level of development, has great possibilities, which go far beyond the natural bonding of women and the sharing of resources. Such a group can be the basis for true study, or the offering of wise guidance, or of service to the community. It can operate even in the most restrictive of environments, because the strength of the light that is within can dissolve normal barriers and resistance.

Light and Conduct

The Lady of Light has the power to transform. In individual women when the light is known, and has been experienced in its different forms, then it can serve to change and inspire. It is, perhaps, the female equivalent of the alchemists' gold, the 'Philosopher's Stone', the elixir which was both a product of transformation itself (made from base matter) and had the power of creating further gold from primitive materials.

The art is to see what needs to be transformed, lifted out of its old state and elevated into a new one. Working with this power of light is not empty moralizing, however. It requires acting out the change in one's own being and conduct so that it can take effect in the appropriate sphere. Let us say, for example, that maybe we would like to change the quality of relationships – marriage and sexual partnership as they are now established in our society. High divorce rates and a high incidence of dissatisfaction among both sexes indicate that we may need to rethink the forms of relationships, the roles we play within them, and the expectations we have of them.

We can look back to a similar situation hundreds of years ago – the taming of knights in the Middle Ages. Some historians say that the introduction of chivalry was entirely the work of women. Apparently the knights were a boorish lot, rude, foul-mouthed, always late for dinner, and showing no respect for their women. The women decided that matters had to change, and, over the course of time, instituted what came to be known as the Courts of Love. The Courts established concepts of chivalry and honour; each knight was to choose and serve one lady. He had to argue his conduct and his love out before the Court, where he was judged by his accomplishment in the arts of love and noble conduct by a panel of women. The Courts ruled as to what was acceptable conduct, and the knights were expected to try to live up to these high standards, not only honouring their women but acting chastely towards them. In those days, marriage was mainly a matter of economy and family; it was not normally possible to marry for love, and indeed the Courts ruled that love and marriage were incompatible. Love was something other, to be cultivated in an intense yet innocent fashion, to inspire deeds of gallantry and to transform the knight into a thinking, feeling being rather than one who picked up his sword without any forethought.

We are not likely to want to return to such a severe division made between love and marriage. We have our own problems, and need our own solutions. The Courts of Love would not have worked if the women had not created the qualities within themselves which those knights could respond to. Their own presence generated the response they were seeking, and the resulting interactions were captured and explored in the code established by the Courts. The story is not about justice; it is not one of righting wrongs, but of acting with love, compassion and wisdom. The light can be used consciously; it is the inspirer of change. In this story its collective, guiding and creative powers were all drawn upon; it is a myth, true in principle, perhaps in literal fact, of how a group of women changed the course of history.

Images

Street Image

You may pass her by unnoticed; her appearance is not out of the ordinary. She sits on the train next to you, a little shabbily dressed in a dark blue overcoat, plain of face and with a hairstyle that is practical rather than glamorous. She is probably older than you. You might recognize her by her kind and open face, a simplicity which you could easily overlook. She is on her way to visit a patient, or teach a group of school children. If you saw her at her work, you might have a very different impression of her, when that gentle, luminous quality turns to a radiant involvement with her task.

Mythic Image

Those who carry the light: Psyche, Florence Nightingale. The star goddesses, such as the Egyptian goddess Nut. The lighters of the way – the female guide who you may encounter on your life's journey, the fairy godmother whose intervention solves all problems. She may be commonplace or dazzling, and can transform herself from one to the other by miraculous means.

Personal Image

What is the light within you, and what does it lead you towards? Does that ideal remain constant, or does it change form as you yourself grow and develop? When do you feel light and contented in your being? (We can use the two meanings of 'light' synonymously here.) Consider what you would most like to transform, and whether the Lady of Light can help you effect that change. Would you work at it with other women, or are you a loner in that respect?

Evolution

Youth

The Lady of Light is not a 'goody goody' saintly child, irritatingly priggish. She is the one who can act simply and unselfishly. You may recognize this when she seems kind and wise beyond her years, but there is no hint of pretentiousness in her manner. It's as if she taps into something greater, and acts with no reservation. The same is found in the young woman, who inspires trust in those she meets. It does not reveal itself all the time; it would seem false if it did.

Maturity

At this time, the woman may find a purposeful role to play. She may serve a cause greater than herself. This could just as well be art as social work or joining a religious movement. She is uninterested in fame; she may attract it, however, and although she finds it annoying, she can turn it to good account for the work she is doing. This woman is unsentimental; she does not want to cloud the light. She knows love, and regards it as the daily currency of life.

Old Age

Her personal life ceases to mean a great deal to her; the main focus of her interests may take on a strong religious flavour. Her powers seem curiously independent of age, and she can call upon extraordinary sources of energy when the need arises. She is loved and visited by many, and is rarely alone.

Manifestations

Gifts

Creative talents in arts, literature, the performing arts. An intuitive knowledge of the future. The ability to forget oneself. The company of other women. Finding a true female guide or teacher.

Finding inner guidance. Love and compassion, given and received.

Trials

Lack of resources to put your visions into practice. Being accused of selfishness. Experiencing ingratitude and hard-heartedness from others. Loss of faith. Losing a sense of direction. The lack of anyone to call upon for guidance.

Rituals and Cults

Sororities of many kinds – social, feminist, scholarly, religious. Doing public service, for example Red Cross work. Private rituals of artistic work, including setting aside time and space to work, preparation of materials, procedure for work. Rituals of personal religious devotion.

The Vision

Of a wisdom which can be found in the smallest gleam, as well as in the fiercest blaze of light.

4

The Queen of the Night

My mother . . . held all the conventional opinions a person was obliged
to have, but then her unconscious personality would suddenly put in an
appearance. That personality was unexpectedly powerful: a sombre,
imposing figure possessed of unassailable authority – and no bones
about it. I was sure that she consisted of two personalities, one innocu-
ous and human, the other uncanny. This other emerged only now and
then, but each time it was unexpected and frightening. She would then
speak as if talking to herself, but what she said was aimed at me and
usually struck to the core of my being, so that I was stunned into
silence . . . There was an enormous difference between my mother's two
personalities. That was why as a child I often had anxiety dreams about
her. By day she was a loving mother, but at night she seemed uncanny.
Then she was like one of those seers who is at the same time a strange
animal, like a priestess in a bear's cave. Archaic and ruthless; ruthless
as truth and nature. At such moments she was the embodiment of what
I have called 'the natural mind'.

(C. G. Jung, *Memories, Dreams, Reflections*, Collins, 1983)

The Queen of the Night is one of the most compelling of the nine
feminine archetypes. She personifies the power and energy that
are unrestricted by convention, the knowledge of forces that
dwell outside the clear, rational light of day; she possesses the
ability to draw upon the tides of night to awaken, attract and
love. She is knowledgeable, magical and primitive. Like all the
nine, her powers can operate either as blind forces or be used
consciously to heighten the quality of life. She is not attractive in
the sense of being charming and graceful. She may shock, or
upset; but to women she represents a power with which they

71

want to be in touch, as their birthright, one that operates naturally in the medium of night, when all the duties of day are left behind.

Night – the Other World

One of the feminist demands in recent years has been to 'reclaim the night'. On the face of it, the phrase refers to the desire to walk freely in cities and streets at night, without fear of attack. However, there may be another implication echoing the age-old drive of women to use the night for expressing a forceful, magical side of nature which the social customs of day prohibit.

The most striking example I have ever seen of this was in Morocco, in North Africa. In this strongly Islamic culture, women may only appear in public draped from head to toe in heavy black robes, with no part of their face showing, except their eyes. The centre of such a woman's life is her home and children. She is expected to obey her husband without question and must never appear unveiled to any man to whom she is not related. One night, at the full moon, we were staying in a small town; it was the height of summer, and the weather as well as the society had begun to seem heavily claustrophobic to us. All was still; there was no noise outside whatsoever. Then a strange din reached our ears, of wailing voices and metallic clashing. We looked out of the window and saw to our astonishment, a procession of women rounding the street corner. Each was unveiled, unrobed, wearing a long dress, her hair free. Together the band of women wailed and sang out, beating cymbals and drums. They danced wildly down the street, abandoning themselves to the night and the moon. In the morning, as I walked again among the modest, secluded women in the town bazaars, the vision of the night seemed like a dream. But we knew it was not, and I have always cherished the strange memory of how those women, who live at such an extreme of personal restriction, had a means of acknowledging their own desire to go free through a custom which celebrated the tides of darkness and the moon.

There is in the feminine psyche a primitive, wild quality, that needs to draw from the power of nature, using the senses of night, when the clear thought and vision of day sleep. When this quality is awakened, it touches the roots of strong emotional drives. Allowed to surface without any control, these can be dangerous and ruthless. On the other hand, when they are totally ignored, life can become artificial and brittle, for the individual or for society in general. We do need order, concern, mutual consideration and careful thought, but not as devices to suppress the darker forces. Night and day are complementary parts of a complete cycle.

It would be tempting to use current psychological labels and call the day the conscious, masculine principle, and the night the unconscious, feminine. There are some useful correspondences here, and the descriptions are helpful in emphasizing the association between the feminine and night, and the subliminal emotional powers. However, although we can keep this association in mind, it does not give us the whole picture.

Nor can we say that only women have access to the powers of the night. Men and women both know what it is to wake in the night and find fierce emotions pounding within them – desire or rage that is not allowed such free rein during the day. We may all experience the compelling and sometimes painful quality of moonlight, or sense the darkness that surrounds us as a palpable presence. Both sexes have need of the night, both have access to it, but it could be said that women represent that force more, and may sometimes be the means through which men make contact with it. Women have to keep it accessible and alive within them, or they are cut off from their roots, whereas men may live almost entirely through the light of day, and keep in touch with night solely through the women in their lives.

Night exposes the vital nerves of emotional drives. These drives may have their foundation in the overriding needs to survive and to reproduce. At base, they have a terrifying volition and ruthlessness. Many a woman who considers herself kind, compassionate and unselfish has been horrified to catch a glimpse of something underlying that, something which is determined to catch and hold a person, which can be jealous and possessive and cares nothing at all for the claims of others. It cares little for social conventions, either. If the 'night forces' are given no safe outlet, no proper channelling, they may erupt with disastrous effect. I have met women who epitomize the 'good mother'; they genuinely love and care for their children and give them a great deal of attention, playing with them and guiding them in a way that most of us feel we can never emulate. All of a sudden, one of these ideal mothers goes off and leaves her children. What has happened? Her husband is shocked, her friends bewildered. She gave no warning signs, and the destruction created in the wake of her departure can be devastating. The immediate cause might be a new lover, or the pursuit of her career, but usually this is just a trigger; the eruptive force is far stronger than that. The underlying reason is that the careful ordering of this woman's life finally choked her, and the survival instinct compelled her to break out before she suffocated completely. Is this to be judged as immoral? Not in the normal sense, I would suggest; it is amoral, in the same way that a thunderstorm breaking is the inevitable outcome of battling elemental forces. For matters to have been different, a far deeper knowledge of those forces would have been required, plus the willingness and ability to handle conflicting tensions long before they built up to breaking point. Perhaps social customs, such as the one that I witnessed in Morocco, are a collective means of doing this. This is in many ways an easier, more convenient option, than the individual taking complete responsibility for her actions. We live in a society which prizes the freedom of the individual, but we are short on means to teach her how to handle it.

In classical mythology we find the example of Aphrodite, who left her dull and lame husband, Hephaestus, for the excitement of an affair with the war-god, Ares, and from then on followed her drives wherever they led her. In his book *She*, Robert A. Johnson associates Aphrodite with 'a primeval, oceanic femininity', which is 'scarcely approachable on normal, conscious, human terms'. He says; 'Every woman has an Aphrodite in her who is easily recognized, her chief characteristics being vanity, conniving lust, fertility, and tyranny when she is crossed.' These forces have no morality as we know it. If we women catch sight of them, we may discover to our alarm that, given suitably tempting circumstances, we would be quite capable of scheming by unscrupulous means to take another woman's husband, or to gain power in a business situation. In her most fundamental expression, the Queen of the Night draws on primitive currents of energy and uses them to fulfil instinctive drives that know little of honour, justice, compassion, or other civilized values.

When women are in touch with this instinctive level of life, they may have deep insights into current situations. Jung remarked that when his mother spoke from this part of her nature she could be unnervingly accurate, and in his book gives several examples of this. Night has its own kind of vision, as if daylight can blind one to certain truths that can only be perceived in the night. Revelations may come in the night, when the mind has shed its normal clutter of reasons and viewpoints. Such knowledge can be very simple, and all the more pertinent for that. It is perhaps this 'night vision' that makes women much more able than men to assess a situation, particularly an emotional one. A woman may know what a man's intentions are towards her, long before he does himself, and can 'pick up' emotional inclinations which he has not yet recognized. It can, however, be difficult for women to retain their self-confidence at this point. A general characteristic of the feminine psyche is to seek confirmation and approval from others, and when these are not forthcoming, it is tempting for the woman to think that she is totally mistaken. But very often her insight is genuine, and time will prove it so.

So far we have discussed the basic power of the night, which can cut through conventions and release emotional energy and revelation. To deny this power is dangerous, for, suppressed, it will find another outlet and may erupt uncontrollably. However, it should not be allowed complete freedom to rule, since it can overwhelm and destroy.

Creatures of the Night

The Queen of the Night has an affinity with the creatures of the night – owls, bats and bright-eyed cats – and, in a more general sense, with all animals. Her association with birds and animals is linked with her ability to use natural drives and the type of primitive but effective forms of perception that these creatures possess. Beasts and birds represent not only the instinctive forces of our being, but also a way of knowing the world that is more extensive than our usual one. They may be able to see in the dark, sense compass direction, and recognize danger. They can run swiftly, fly, go underground and display extraordinary agility. Many nocturnal creatures are hunters, which again accords with our Queen of the Night, who can use her powers in a predatory fashion.

Since very ancient times, there has been a symbolic representation of woman found in many cultures, known as the 'Mistress of the Beasts'. She may be portrayed with lions, bulls, birds, serpents, or other creatures, and she is shown dominating them, but rarely struggling with them or slaying them. She may have wings, or she may ride in a chariot drawn by wild animals. Such emblems, in their different manifestations, seem to imply that women have the power to empathize with the animal kingdom, to tame wild creatures, and use their strength and attributes. The root connection of men with animals is by trial of strength – by hunting, or wrestling with animals, to master them. The female way is to know and to tame. Indeed, it is thought that the first domestic animals may have originated as wild babies brought home by the hunters for their womenfolk to rear. It is not necessarily a soft option to tame wild animals, for to do so involves understanding their nature, being at one with it and drawing it into new forms of behaviour. Sometimes it is dangerous; even so-called domestic creatures can revert to their wild, savage state. I have a sizeable chunk of my left thumb missing due to an early encounter with a vicious horse, and I was already highly experienced at looking after horses when this happened. One of my cats, unassuming and docile by nature most of the time, turns into a wild tiger if I have to hold her still to give her medicine. I am hardly in mortal danger from her, but she has drawn blood on numerous occasions. Her tameness drops away like a spring moult, and her primitive survival instincts supplant everything else. The Queen of the Night must understand these instincts, if she is to have control over them; she must know her own wildness, and sense within herself the vigilance of the owl and the cunning of the fox before she can bring them into her domain. By knowing these wild creatures and their attributes, she contacts the same powers in herself, and may learn to use them.

In Mozart's opera *The Magic Flute*, there is a Queen of the Night, a sinister but magnificent figure, who demands that birds be caught and brought to her every day. She, too, is an ambivalent figure. Is she the evil mother, who tries to prevent her daughter Pamina from discovering her true father, Sarastro, and entering the Temple of Wisdom? Is she a wronged, outcast queen? Or is she the dark, instinctive force which Pamina must acknowledge and cease to accept unquestioningly, separating herself from it so that she can grow and begin her life's journey?

In connection with the Queen of the Night and her birds, I was lucky enough to see an example of such interaction recently when I watched a woman falconer give a demonstration of her art. She worked with several hawks and falcons, putting each through its paces according to its maturity and natural ability. None was working against its basic instincts, but with each bird she had created something more. She used the cry of her voice to draw them to her, allowing them first to fly away and then encouraging them to swoop back at the height of their arc of flight. As they became confident, she moved them into faster and more daring exhibitions, inciting them to dive skilfully for a titbit or a 'lure'. With the 'lure', a dummy prey swung around on a cord, it was particularly obvious that the birds were enjoying the game with her, rising to the challenge and the chance to show their prowess. The falconer had authority and poise, she remained in control of the whole operation, and her attention was with the bird at each second of its flight – all while delivering a running commentary! Falconry is not a sport confined to women, but on this occasion I felt I had seen the perfect emblem for the 'Mistress of the Beasts'. Her sympathetic command over the birds epitomized feminine power over animals, for there was no supremacy of strength involved, but a superb understanding of their nature, and a trust between bird and owner. Several of those hawks could have taken off and never returned, but they did not; the falconer could rely on the training and the care she had given them. They were still creatures of the wild, but had been brought into the domain of the human without sacrificing their natural powers.

The Queen of the Night, in her representation with the creatures of the night, is not at their mercy, nor does she completely civilize and tame their natures. She rules them, and it is a rule based on their trust of her and her knowledge of them. What do these creatures represent? In one sense, they are the strong passions and urges that I have described as coming from 'the roots of emotion'. They are wild, and sometimes fierce – desire, anger, fear, protectiveness, and a basic form of love. It is difficult even to name them, for I sense that they are urges and longings that spring up from the deep, like streams of water gathering in the darkness below ground before they emerge through the rock into the light of day. They provide a kind of basic emotional energy which we need in order to keep relationships alive, and to put energy into our life's work. Women tell themselves frequently that they should not show anger, or be jealous, or desire power. The psychologists have plenty to say about this, about how the repressed emotion can then be projected on to a partner, or cause a kind of dual way of life to develop, where a woman may be sweet and lovely on the surface but grasping and rapacious beneath. As women, we need to accept that we can be fierce, cunning and predatory before we can start to use these energies in a constructive way.

There are many ways in which these emotional drives can be channelled, and I could not hope to name more than a few of them. They can go into whatever activity it is in your life that is to do with handling unruly forces: animals, problem children, emergency work, or sports that have an edge of danger to them, such as rock-climbing or hang-gliding. In relationships they can go into the challenging and testing of a man's intention, and into the releasing of inhibitions in the sexual act. They find an obvious outlet in the act of childbirth, and the protection of the young baby. They can go into the furtherance of a chosen goal, and here something of the difference between the 'Mistress of the Beasts' and the male hunter can be glimpsed, for whereas a man may wrestle openly with every difficulty on the way, women can use more precision and grace, choosing moments with care, sensing the atmosphere, and employing only as much force as is necessary. The drives can go into the performing arts, transformed into the will to communicate, to wake up an audience, to escalate the level of power being conveyed through the speech, song or dance. Training in skills such as singing or dancing often seems to involve not just acquiring technique, but opening a way through to the basic level of power so that it can 'fuel' the performance. Teachers have to struggle to break down a pupil's conceptions of what is 'beautiful', 'lovely' and nice to watch in order to release the real potential. Going through a period of artistic training can involve a frightening leap into the unknown – into the 'night' where one's carefully constructed notions will dissolve and something much greater, more awesome, take their place.

As well as representing primitive emotional drives, the night creatures suggest extended abilities of perception. It is possible to develop what may be rudimentary, animal-like senses in ourselves. These may involve knowing when another person is nearby, without visible or auditory clue, or sensing compass direction, or 'seeing' over a long distance. There are many reported cases of 'primitive' peoples knowing each other's whereabouts over distances of several hundred miles. Night symbolizes the dying-down of normal paths of perception, in order that others may grow stronger. These may be purely physical, in the way that smell and touch become more intense in darkness, or they may be more on the psychic level. I have often learned through dreams – frequently just floating snippets, as it were –

things which I could not have learnt through my normal perceptions. These may be very simple things, such as 'seeing' that a friend will be getting in touch shortly, or knowing what is coming in tomorrow's post. Sometimes they can have a mythical dimension, images that shed a new light on traditions of wisdom or legend. Recently, just before I woke up, I had an insight that I perceived as being connected with the Celtic tradition; I 'saw' that animal sacrifice in Celtic mythology was a way of buying interaction with the world of spirits, the souls of the animals being the currency used. There was no cruelty attached to this in their eyes; it was a simple means to procure the necessary connection with the invisible, supernatural world. This took no longer than a couple of seconds to see and understand, a near-abstract image accompanied by a few words. Such a realization may have been fuelled by my existing knowledge of mythology (though it is not detailed in this respect), but it arose in a form that conveyed more in two seconds than two hours of normal thought could produce. In my own case, I think that when the normal clamour and technicolour impressions of the day are not bombarding my system, then other impressions are able to make their presence known. The veil of ordinary thinking drops away; associations can surface from a deeper level. It is more than just the onset of literal night; it is a night of the normal senses, allowing other means of knowing to arise.

In describing these ways of sensing, I am probably going beyond the bounds of what pertains especially to the feminine, since these are basic human abilities. It is possible that women are, on the whole, more receptive to acknowledging them, and will use them more readily. Because of their role in childbearing, women are natural candidates for empathetic relationships, and the boundaries between 'self' and 'other' may be less marked in the female. It is the normal concept of 'where I stop' that keeps out some of these more unusual and far-flung perceptions, or prevents their being recognized. A pregnant woman, and even one with a young baby, can no longer be so sure 'where she stops'.

Women are also very quick to pick up emotional atmospheres,

and to sense the quality in a room or building. The Queen of the Night is good at 'house-hunting' and knows almost immediately whether she will feel at ease in a particular abode. Once again, although men are capable of this too, the ability is less marked, and many will rely on their women to pick up the intangible clues, or to decode their own shadowy impressions for them.

Flying in the Dark

Finally, in this chapter, I will suggest some of the ways in which the qualities of the Queen of the Night can be used by women. The examples which I give are only hints and pointers, and parallels can be found in many different areas of life, from the mundane to the mystical. The qualities of the Queen of the Night, as with the other eight archetypes, can be discovered in a variety of personal and cultural contexts; none of the Nine can ever be pinned down to one final form. This applies especially to the Queen of the Night, for by her very nature she is shadowy, changeable and deceptive.

Her ability to change form is illustrated in the quotation which opened this chapter, where Jung describes how his mother seemed to take on another shape and quality at night. He implies that her form became larger, less defined, a combination of woman and animal. It is common for children to sense this underlying quality in their mothers, particularly during night-time visits; a child may respond to its mother's presence with a cry of: 'Go away, you witch! I want my mummy!'

A daughter knows the dark, night side of her mother, because of the special link that is forged between them and the way that the mother's nature may be reflected in the daughter's. The daughter may refuse to accept the mother's professed self-image, sensing the pride that lurks beneath meekness, for instance. And the mother may castigate the daughter for her unruly behaviour, at the same time betraying a sly triumph when she relates how uncontrollable and wilful the girl is. She may subtly encourage in her daughter all the characteristics she would like to express openly herself, but dare not.

The 'shape-changing' qualities of the Queen of the Night may be associated with the moon, which waxes from dark to full and declines again. A woman can change from a bright, outgoing mood one day to a dark and brooding one the next. This will produce different responses as both people and animals around her may react differently to each 'phase'. The woman is quite capable of using these varying qualities to draw out particular types of response; she may do this instinctively, or consciously, and for a variety of reasons. Very often the 'bright'-faced moon beams out energy and optimism to others, whereas the dark side is a drawing-in of forces to itself. Women may feed their husbands or lovers with energy and then, after a while, change tack, deciding that it is time to draw the tide of emotional response towards themselves. The 'dark'-moon state may often be recognized when you are in conversation with a woman, by a lack of signalled response even though she is listening to you. You may sense that your words are tumbling out into a kind of void. It is through this means that women can pull and attract others and draw into themselves energies from external sources.

Described in this way, the process sounds primitive and predatory. It can be so – certain women have a perpetual 'devouring' quality – but it is a natural process, echoed in the menstrual cycle, and in the moon's waxing and waning, and it can be used to positive effect, regulating the ebb and flow of relationships and opening up pathways of communication. We speak, after all, of 'drawing out' a person, meaning encouraging his or her true feelings and thoughts to surface.

The 'shape-changing' can also be achieved through letting go of the normal ways of keeping up appearances. I mentioned earlier that the Queen of the Night can cut through conventions. When we choose to drop some of the social and individual details by which we are recognized, then we acquire a different form. Our everyday image is built up from a mass of little details – dress, social manners, tone of voice, and so on. Most of these have been evolved to adapt to the conventions of society and the expectations of others. Although they have an individual stamp, they are really only accessories – and we can change or discard some of them. It is possible to use such changes of form to escape from existing snares. Other people's assessments of us are usually based on what they think they know about us. We have an image which is founded on their mental and emotional reactions. If we change some of those responses, then it is likely that the people who have used and relied on them will not 'know' us any more, and their demands will have no further effect.

Changing inner state can be used actively, for a specific effect. It is part of the training in magical traditions that participants learn to take up roles and then drop them again after the working session is over. In such traditions, when a session is in progress, one or more of the participants may be designated as 'guardians', to protect the room or space that is being used, checking on a mental as well as a physical plane that it is not being intruded upon. To be 'on guard' under such circumstances is not simply a matter of standing rigidly to attention, brandishing a suitably ferocious weapon. Just as an actor has to take on a role as an inner state, rather than relying solely on costume and a loud voice, so, in this case, guarding is achieved primarily through an inner attitude of alertness, watchfulness and a readiness to act swiftly. Its purpose is best served if the person concerned can take up this attitude, be with it for as long as is required, and then let it go again when stepping back into ordinary life, then there is no risk of becoming over-identified with it. Such roles, far from being confined to magical rites and ceremonies, have their counterparts in everyday life. A playground supervisor is a guardian while she is on duty, acting with authority, keeping an eye out for trouble, intervening before tears or blood are shed! But if she takes her job too seriously, and acts in this way towards her own children at home, she will lose the intimacy of the relationship and seem a very impersonal and unkind mother.

To go into the 'night' betokens a willingness to go into the unknown. The outlines shown by daylight are obscured; shapes and colours are different, if indeed they can be perceived at all. It is a world of potential. It may be potential ecstasy, fear, love, anger, pain or communion. There is no knowing in advance.

The Queen of the Night has knowledge of her domain, but her knowledge has been built up by allowing the quality of the dark to touch her, and the nature of its creatures to awaken a response in her own being. As she flies through the dark, or gallops on the horse of night, she is using different skills from those of our daytime world.

A woman's way of learning to 'fly in the dark' is an individual one, for it must come by discovering her own source of power, the potential of her emotional and sexual drives. Just to go out into the night can give a sense of this; night is not empty darkness – the night can be warm, or stormy, still or windy, and the darkness is charged by this and has a changing life of its own. As a teenager, I often felt impelled to imagine that I was running or flying with the wind in the dark. This gave me a great sense of freedom – and, just occasionally, I did hurtle down the street at night!

Adolescent girls do not yet have the lid of society fitting tightly on their bubbling psyches – and we have, therefore, the phenomenon of frenzied screaming at rock stars, or wild dancing, as an outlet for some of this 'night energy'. The Moroccan women I spoke of earlier had a means of giving it some expression. A lighter-hearted example is found in an Elizabethan song, 'Hark all you Ladies', by Thomas Campion. It begins:

> Hark all you ladies that do sleep,
> The fairy queen, Proserpina,
> Bids you awake, and pity them that weep.
> You may do in the dark what the day doth forbid;
> Fear not the dogs that bark; night will have all hid.

The call, it emerges, is to unbridled love, something that this sedate day-time society was not willing to permit. It is likely that many secret societies of women have met at night, and in Western Europe the controversial tradition of witchcraft certainly uses night-time as the appropriate part of the day for work.

Exposing oneself to the night can not only have a powerful personal effect, but, in modern cities, be very dangerous for a woman. Nonetheless, as a recent television documentary showed, women still rise to this challenge. An elderly lady, a writer of crime-stories, was featured; for years she has taken regular night walks, striding out for miles through the city of London, observant of everything around her. She talks to a number of the people she encounters, the late-night revellers, shiftworkers, and the homeless. On the programme, she commented that her excursions into the world of night give her some very special insights and material which she is then able to use in her novels. Apparently she has never once run into personal danger, and perhaps the clarity of her intention, and the careful planning of her route each night, have helped in this respect. Amusingly, the one threat she had encountered was from another 'Queen of the Night', a grossly huge woman, who only felt able to emerge into the world in the dead of night, and was enraged to find another woman watching her take her secret walk in the darkness.

Each of us has to make her own journey into the world of night. We go there with different motivations: to discover knowledge, love, or power. Entering that world with conscious intention reduces the risk that we shall be lost, or overwhelmed, but we must still be ready to face the unexpected.

Images

Street Image

She emerges from a shadowy underpass, dressed in black leather. She likes to shock; from current trends, the Gothic style pleases her; in earlier years it would have been punk, or beatnik. her hair is teased into spikes and her face a pallid mask of make-up, livid colours on her eyes and mouth. There is an aura of sinister mystery about her appearance. She takes an Alsatian dog around with her; it will make you nervous if she doesn't have it on a lead. You don't know where she's going, and it's better not to ask.

Mythic Image

In full view, she is splendid, but terrifying. You invoke her at your peril; she may appear in a chariot drawn by wild beasts rushing through the darkness, suddenly descending upon you. She has cunning combined with ruthlessness. There are few secrets that you can keep from her. Women of darkness: Lady Macbeth, Mozart's Queen of the Night, even Cathy, in Emily Brontë's *Wuthering Heights*, with her fierce loves and hates which cannot be bound by the rules of day.

Personal Image

Where do you seek danger? When do you enjoy taking risks? There is something in you that loves the wild, the primitive; you will pursue it even at the cost of what you cherish. How far will you go with convention before you are compelled to break out of it? What does darkness mean to you, and what powers can you call upon to see and know when the light of day has gone?

Evolution

Youth

The Queen of the Night is a natural rebel in youth. Maybe she is also fearful, at least when she is younger; power appears as the witch, the nightmare, the fascinating but terrifying darkness, and is not yet recognized as part of her own psyche. In adolescent rebellion, she is tempted to go beyond the boundaries – the law, the commands of her parents, and the expectations of friends. She trespasses on forbidden ground.

Maturity

The woman has learnt to use her power now, and wields it in her job, her partnership, with her family. She draws on subterranean forces to subjugate and control. She knows that if she uses power there is a price to pay – you cannot be loved by everyone, you may stand beyond the normal bounds of acceptability. Every now and then she feels the urge to do something exciting and out of character; people are never quite sure what to expect from her.

Old Age

The classic picture of the eccentric old lady, living with a houseful of cats. She cares little for appearance and does not abide by the usual social rules. She eats, sleeps, and takes exercise when she pleases; her timetable may be geared to the night rather than the day. She can enjoy the last freedom to be as she is; her pursuits may seem strange, but after her death it may be discovered that her treasured collection – of old cups, pressed flowers, or newspaper cuttings – is quite priceless.

Manifestations

Gifts

A natural affinity with animals and birds. Love of wild places. The ability to see through pretence. Adaptable body rhythms, as easily nocturnal as diurnal. The need for only little sleep. Psychic gifts, such as clairvoyance and telepathy. Opportunities for adventure. Freedom from normal routine.

Trials

Captivity of any kind; being confined in an artificial environment, or being forced to conform to a suffocating set of social rules and conventions. Accidents; danger from natural sources, such as animals, storms, landfall etc.

Rituals and Cults

Secret magical societies of women, including witchcraft. The tradition of the wise woman, as seer and healer. Women as trainers of animals – for example, horses, guard dogs, birds of prey. Both social and private rituals that celebrate night, moon, and the changing tides.

The Vision

The power of instinct, fierce and primitive, and the knowledge that it brings.

5

The Great Mother

I suddenly told them that I had to push, the urge was absolutely OVERPOWERING, quite unbelievable. This was about 8 a.m. I was told I couldn't, but said to hell with it, I've got to, so they said OK. It was very easy to push, but the contractions were still very bad, especially in my thighs.

I could hear myself groaning like an old pig! and the doctor told me to use all that energy I was expending on the noise to push with!

I felt a burning, splitting sensation, and Dick told me to look as the head had crowned, and I could see she had dark hair. I was told not to push then, and I saw the midwife go to cut the cord, and finally it clicked what all the fuss had been about.

I found it very difficult not to push then, and although I tried the puff, puff, blow it didn't help, and I had to pant. Suddenly I just couldn't stand it any longer and said I've GOT to push and she came out like a champagne cork at 8.15 a.m.

I looked down and saw her lying between my legs, she was so small. I was told I'd got a little girl, then I heard her crying.

(From a mother's 'labour report', National Childbirth Trust, 1974)

The act of giving birth creates the separation of mother and child. Is it at this point that a woman becomes a mother? It is both the mother and baby who are born out of that moment? Or does motherhood start further back, at the moment of conception? Perhaps it can be traced even deeper in the past – we can go back to the time when the woman first attracted the man whose child she will later bear, or to the onset of her menstruation, when her body signalled its readiness for pregnancy. Perhaps we could go back still further, to the event of her own birth, and even into an intra-uterine existence, for it is at this time that the ovaries and all the eggs are formed in the female. A baby girl emerges into the world with the pattern for her future possible children already laid within her body.

In thinking about motherhood, we also begin to consider the nature of time, for the two are linked. Motherhood brings about an affirmation of time. The apparent timelessness of gestation and life in the womb is followed by the moment of entry into the world, which is the beginning of the time-span of one human life. Death is implicit in birth. An awareness of a longer span of time also comes with motherhood, a sense of being connected to both past and future through a succession of births. It has been known for a woman going into labour to suddenly perceive the connection between herself, her mother, mother's mother, all the mothers of her line stretching back to the beginnings of time, and all the daughters that will follow after. A vision awesome in its scale, sustaining in its strength. And there is still another way of understanding time, which is that when a mother gives birth, she is giving birth to time itself, to a 'life-time', and she is thus in some sense beyond time itself. Certainly, it is common to lose all track of time in labour; the intensity of the last stages seem to take place in another dimension. The individual has only one span of time, one life, but the mother can give birth to multiple lives. Her relationship with one child can seem timeless, eternal, until she is pregnant and gives birth again. Then this spell may be broken, for both her and the child, since the new baby represents yet another time-cycle which she carries and gives birth to.

Exploring ideas of motherhood can plunge us right into the heart of mystical philosophy as well as into the practical world of child rearing. Here, as with others of the Nine, I shall try to touch on both the inner meaning and the outer realities of the Great Mother. She is potentially the most cliché-ridden of the nine archetypes. Archaeologists, anthropologists and psychologists are all guilty of shovelling up a multitude of references to the feminine and labelling the heap as the 'Great Mother'. Just as it is easy to put the tag 'ritual object' on any unknown prehistoric artefact, so, too, it is easy to class any mythical or artistic representation of the female as the universal mother.

In this chapter, therefore, I may omit some of the standard descriptions of the Great Mother, which the reader can easily find elsewhere. I would rather draw on ideas which seem to be meaningful in the present context and which offer opportunities for further exploration – not the babies already born and growing up, but ones in the making! The fecundity of the Great Mother gives rise to numerous ways in which she can be defined.

The State of Motherhood

A young woman once interviewed on the radio was asked whether she felt that working as a cleaner was beneath her. Her reply was: 'I'm a mother – so nothing is beneath me!' Motherhood is a great leveller. Pregnancy demolishes any attempts at personal elegance, as we bulge and waddle along. Individuality counts for little as the nurse in the antenatal clinic brightly calls us 'Mother', and the doctor treats us as if we were half-witted. After the birth, any desires we may have to rise above the physical mire are crushed as nappy-changing, spurting milk and sticky fingers involve us well and truly in the messy side of life. As hair gets tied back, so nail varnish comes off and old, stain-absorbing clothes go on. Unless a mother divorces herself completely from the essential tasks of child care, handing over her baby to others, her role will keep her in touch with the most basic elements of life!

There is more to motherhood than this, of course; it is a source of vital feelings and responses which come about no other way. And sometimes, despite the squalor and the squalling, even the popular, pretty image of mother and child may come into focus. But not for long. My husband and I had photographs taken of ourselves with our firstborn when he was a week or so old; in the pictures we all look happy and contented. The serenity, however, is an illusion: the secret lay in the photographer's skill in catching the few fleeting moments when our son was not roaring his head off.

The physical process of motherhood changes a woman's life. The capacity for motherhood is a capacity for transformation; by accepting new life within our bodies, allowing it to grow, giving birth to it and rearing it, we ourselves are irrevocably changed. Such changes are both physical and mental. Giving birth has a quality of absolute and fundamental reality. That pregnancy should end in birth has an inevitability which is matched only by the inevitability that life will end in death. It can be awesome, and frightening. Some days after my daughter's birth, our second child, I experienced a very deep sense of grief mixed with my joy, as I recognized that this small and perfect human life that had been born must grow old and die. However much we try to stave off the raw realities of birth and childcare – with pain-killing drugs, for instance – they must somehow be taken into account, or they will force their way through into consciousness in even more painful ways. It is often found that women who, for whatever reason, are not able to participate actively in giving birth, experience difficulty in relating to their babies later on. Fortunately nowadays the need for women to be wholly involved in the birth process is more widely recognized, and it is better understood that technology is not the only priority for a safe and acceptable birth. Theories of maternal instinct and mother–child bonding are emotionally loaded, and constantly being re-appraised; although lack of consistency in approach brings its own problems, at least this shows how vital the issue is. The challenge in our modern world is to use medical techniques that will preserve the life of the baby and the health of the mother, yet still allow women to respond to the natural forces of childbirth, so that they may really feel they have given birth, rather than having a baby taken out of them. Birth is the acknowledgement of separation; without this, mother and child cannot know each other properly.

I mentioned that motherhood is a great leveller, and it is true that it can break down all sorts of social barriers. Women with babies have something in common and can strike up a conversation, and the old and the young find it easy to talk to one another when there is a baby in the picture. Motherhood can be a remarkable giver of confidence, and it can also demolish arrogance. A girl who has been shy or awkward can become quite self-possessed as she cares for her new baby. Another, a highly qualified career woman, can find herself completely thrown by trying to juggle the demands of a baby, husband and household. Her less intellectual sister next door may be tranquilly watching television, an infant asleep beside her and a stew bubbling on the stove, while the first-class honours graduate hunts frantically for a clean nappy as the baby howls and the telephone rings. Mothers can give each other confidence, but on the other hand, all sorts of nastiness and competitiveness can grow up between women when motherhood is in question. The Great Mother aspect of our nature makes us insist on knowing and doing best. Achieving a perfect birth, a contented baby or a streamlined schedule can give rise to a smug self-satisfaction. A group of women talking about motherhood may either find some way of adjusting their differing statements so that they are *all* right, or else become locked in bitter disagreement, which is no less vitriolic even if it is not openly expressed. Women usually venture their views on child care in order to be assured that they are right; they fiercely resent being told that they are wrong. Each mother–child relationship is triumphantly unique, and hence any argument that has reached loggerheads may be concluded with, 'Well, *I* know what's right for *my* child!'

Confidence is an essential ingredient in happy child rearing, and many experts on child care recognize that where such confidence is found, it should not be attacked, as it is the foundation of the mother–child relationship. Sheila Kitzinger, anthropologist and authority on methods of natural childbirth, found on a field trip to the Caribbean that if she questioned women too strongly about the reasons why they did this or that with their babies, their easy confidence would suddenly start to crumble. Our changing society, and the advance of medicine, have, however, forced us to ask questions about why we do certain things, and to suggest new methods. A general lack of confidence is noticeable as a result. What was appropriate in our mothers' day is not necessarily so in ours, and therefore we look for new sources of guidance, since instruction of daughters by mothers is less readily acceptable than it was. Hence we have come to rely more and more on books, classes and professional advice to tell us how to give birth and bring up children. Ideally, such techniques should assist our own instincts and innate strength, rather than taking over from them.

Accepting Motherhood

The term, the 'Great Mother', is often associated with primitive and prehistoric carvings of large, shapeless women. These have no pretensions to beauty as we normally conceive it; they evoke the fecund, swelling, expansive, receptive aspect of womanhood. Such statues represent the anonymous, all-powerful, all-containing 'Mother'. Modern echoes of this are evoked with hideous pottery mugs and lurid birthday cards inscribed 'To Mother'. Which mother? Whose mother? It does not matter; they are dedicated just to 'Mother'. As women, we can feel a dread of being overtaken by this archetype. Something of our individuality is swept away by it, and a reluctance to have children can often have its roots in this fear. To become mother to a child is to step into a universal role, to be type-cast by the world at large and even by one's own children. Small children have strong ideas about what mothers do or do not do; my own adolescent children are very worried about what I might do in public to embarrass them. Women can be frightened of losing their looks, their intelligence, their jobs, their youth, or anything else that they prize, through having babies; even though none of this may happen in fact, the fear arises from sensing the real force of motherhood, which ruthlessly dissolves self-image and cherished convictions. Welcoming motherhood means welcoming change.

To some extent, it means allowing the Great Mother archetype to flourish within ourselves. I have noticed that on photographs the faces of women giving birth look remarkably alike. It is as if the individual features give way to a universal picture. At the moment of the baby's expulsion, the face has an expansive quality, a complete openness. Before that, during the labour, there is a primitive fierceness, a total involvement with an overpowering experience. The act of giving birth strips away much of the personal life; labouring women may cease to notice who is in the room, or to hear what is said. One's normal identity loses its hold and is replaced by the feeling: 'I am the act of giving birth'. What happens afterwards is variable both from woman to woman and from birth to birth. Emotions may come flooding in as soon as the baby is born, or there may be a sense of detachment which lasts hours or days. The transition back to 'self', as we normally think of it, may not be immediate.

As well as accepting the role of motherhood, a woman who has a child is also faced with the need to accept facts about time, and ageing. A mother is in some sense outside time to her baby, and young children usually have no realistic idea of how old their mothers are. A mother can seem both ageless and as old as the hills to her child. Again, this can be difficult to face as we are maybe used to thinking of ourselves as 'dynamic twenty-five', 'attractive thirty-four', or even 'youthful forty-three'. Our children's growing-up time will be measured alongside our own years. This will provide a continual series of shocks when we realize that, in our terms, it is 'only a few years' since the infant gurgled in its cot, but the 'infant', who is now almost grown up, properly considers it to be 'a lifetime ago'. The glowing young mother can also become a reluctant young grandmother rather early on. We may be young to ourselves, but we will always be old to our children.

Some women will happily abandon themselves to complete involvement in the role of 'mother', for several years. They may even make a permanent identification with it, and this can cause problems when the children leave home. It seems dangerous to centre your life on any one of the nine archetypes; they are aspects of the feminine, not its totality. In order to create an individual life in the world, we should use them as colours on an artist's palette, to paint our own picture. Sometimes we may use much more of one colour than another; this is natural since different demands and opportunities arise at each phase of life. If, in a sense, the Great Mother presides over the physical act of childbirth, then it is wise to submit to her demands during pregnancy, birth and the infancy of the child. The mother herself needs to go into a kind of protective womb; she is vulnerable, and requires care and support. Trying to 'carry on as usual' during this critical phase is likely to set up conflict, and can be a way of trying to evade the realities of birth. If a woman allows the Great Mother her dues – to establish her presence within her – she will make the transition into new or renewed motherhood more easily.

I always feel slightly alarmed when I hear a pregnant woman describing the future with relentless certainty: work until the eighth month, three months off, a holiday abroad, back to work, and so on. We cannot count on any of this. High blood pressure may force her to stop work early; the baby may need special care and, more importantly, she cannot be sure how she will feel after the birth of the child. She may be ecstatic and radiant; she may on the other hand feel tired and depressed. Naturally this can radically affect her choices, as to whether she takes her job back again, for instance, or gives herself time and space to adjust to the demands of motherhood. However safe the processes of childbirth become, an aim that we would all agree upon, I think, its course can never be determined with absolute certainty. Choosing to get pregnant means letting go of control. With my own two children, I felt cheerful and reasonably well during the first pregnancy; the bonding process with the baby was immediate and passionate, but nine months later I was seeking medical help for exhaustion. With the second, the pregnancy was miserable and I felt ill most of the time. The birth was fine, the bonding process took a couple of days longer, and I felt such a surge of energy rushing back into my system that I decided to open a shop at the end of the first week, and did in fact do so six weeks after the birth. I could not have predicted any of this.

Plenty of women remain childless, through choice or necessity. It is easy to say one of two things: either that such women find an outlet for their mothering instincts through other channels, or that they have no place for the mothering urge within their lives. Such descriptions may have truth in them, but I think there is yet another way of looking at the situation. The Great Mother represents the lineage of women. She is the great chain of mothers and daughters, her life stretching from the dawn of time to an inconceivably distant future. Every woman is connected to that lineage, whether or not she furthers it through physical reproduction. If we imagine the Great Mother as a huge, strong tree, then the childless women are like the very tips of the branches; they create the tracery of twigs, its outline, while the mothers form the wood that is still growing, their daughters pushing out beyond them into the space around.

Life and Death

The Great Mother is a symbol of the way in which life is brought into being in the world, from the first hidden appearance of a spark of life in the covered darkness to the birth of a fully formed being. But she is also the symbol for a return of life into that darkness. This can be seen in two ways. Firstly, as the ending of one individual life, dissolving back into a cauldron of greater life; this process is the domain of the Great Mother as archetype. Secondly, in the devouring quality of a human or animal mother when she is driven to reclaim the life to which she has given birth.

With the first instance, we touch on the mysteries of death; we should be careful not to make too much of the Great Mother as a goddess of birth and death; she is not the originator of these but rather the one who shapes the coming and guides the going of each life. She is no more the cause of life than any of the other eight; she is a representative of the forces that govern our lives in terms of the feminine psyche. But perhaps her presence can be witnessed at the time of death. There is a phase preceding death – perhaps moments before, perhaps even as much as a year before – when the individual life seems to dissolve and to begin to be absorbed back into the collective life. This can sometimes be sensed in elderly persons who are approaching the end. The personality, something built up by interaction in the world, may become rigid and show signs of extreme wear – it is like a mask which is becoming stiff and cumbersome – but the spirit is becoming freer, disengaging from the normal functions of everyday life. If one looks only at the outer signs, one may see a cantankerous, dotty old person, but in the soul something very different may be perceived.

We, the living, may glimpse something of our common origin when we witness the death of another. Recently, I picked up a young bird which one of my cats had caught; I held it in my hands in the hope that it might survive. The shock had been too great, though, and its heart went into convulsions. And then came a moment when I was aware that its personal life was dissolving, and I could somehow perceive that a greater life, a kind of group 'bird soul' was taking over, for want of a better phrase. Just after this, the creature went into its death throes, and the impression of death as something dark and fierce, pulling all that was left of life out of the little body, was horrible indeed. But my observation told me that the moments of personal suffering were over before that; the bird's individuality had been reclaimed. If we ascribe this to the archetype of the Great Mother, then it seems that her presence at the time of death reveals one of her most compassionate aspects.

In the second instance of the link between the mother and the return to darkness, it can be seen how the mother in our everyday world stands as a figure in which the individual may lose him or herself. The child runs to its mother to be comforted, and for a minute or two is lost in her. Grown men are still aware of this potential loss of self, and many have an instinctive fear of the 'devouring' quality of women, since it can threaten their personal integrity. The growing boy has to learn to separate himself from his mother, and establish himself as a person in his own right. Sometimes this involves heavy conflict, and he may ever after be sensitive to the threat posed by powerful women who try to dominate him. In the animal kingdom, when breeding conditions are not right, the mothers of certain species, such as rabbits, will eat their new-born young. It is a gruesome and appalling thought to us; it seems a reversal of the true principles of nature, and yet, how can it be, when it occurs as a common phenomenon? Even the apparent eating of children provokes a shudder of revulsion, as in the habits of the Nile crocodile. She lays her eggs, and when the babies are ready to hatch they call out a warning to her that they are coming out. As soon as they are born, she takes them into her huge jaws where they lie in pouches as she carries them back down the river. This image of the crocodile seemingly swallowing her offspring evokes a real primitive horror in human emotions; it touches the fear of being taken back and devoured by the mother from whom we must grow away.

Knowledge in the Darkness of the Womb

The womb is a dark space, a container for life. It may have a seed growing within it, or be empty. It may hold within it the memories of the lives it has fostered, and the foreknowledge of the forms that will be rooted there. The womb represents the very first place in which life takes form. It is not surprising to find, therefore, that the womb has a key role in many religious teachings.

It is a central doctrine of Christianity that the womb of the Virgin Mary became the means by which God descended into human form and was born as Jesus Christ. In the present context of the nine archetypes, a description given in a Gnostic text is particularly interesting. The work seems to date from the transitional period between Old Testament Judaism and Christianity. It describes the ways in which a Saviour, an 'imperishable illuminator', may be born:

> And the [ninth] kingdom says of him
> that from the nine Muses one separated away. She came
> to a high mountain and spent [some] time seated there,
> so that she desired herself alone in order to become
> androgynous. She fulfilled her desire and became
> pregnant from her desire.
> He was born.
> The angels who were over the desire nourished him.
> And he received glory there and power.

And thus he came to the water.
> ('The Apocalypse of Adam', from *The Nag Hammadi Library*,
> edited by James M. Robinson)

Christianity is not the only religion to suggest that divinity may be born on earth through a chosen, sacred womb. Legends of the birth of the Buddha describe how the Great Being, the disincarnate Buddha, surveyed the ranks of living women to find one perfect enough to be his mother. Having chosen such a one, he appeared to her as a vision of a white elephant, and conception took place as he struck her womb with his trunk. Whereas Christianity stresses the sacredness of Christ's birth through the fact of Mary's virginity, Buddhism gives emphasis to the idea that the mother has transcended normal human existence by fostering the Buddha in her womb:

And within her womb she could distinguish the Future Buddha, like a white thread passed through a transparent jewel. And whereas a womb that has been occupied by a Future Buddha is like the shrine of a temple, and can never be occupied or used again, therefore it was that the mother of the Future Buddha died when he was seven days old, and was reborn in the Tusita heaven.

> (Henry Clarke Warren, *Buddhism in Translations*,
> Harvard University Press, 1963)

The price to pay for being a vessel for divine birth seems to be rather a high one.

In allowing life to grow in the womb, a woman is partly handing over to powers outside her conscious control. Religious doctrine may describe these powers as the holy spirit descended into material form; everyday terminology may call them the forces of Nature. Perhaps we can find something of both in the process. In the early stages of pregnancy, or even at conception itself, a mother may become aware of a living presence within her body, sensing its spirit before there are any physical symptoms at all. She may have dreams which clearly show her initiation into pregnancy, and even the sex of the unborn child. But although we may have a spiritual or mental knowledge of the pregnancy, the actual physical development of the baby in the womb has to lie beyond our conscious control. We may try to assist the pregnancy by following a good diet and receiving medical care, but we cannot make the baby grow, any more than we can manufacture the growth of a plant. We can only provide the best conditions possible for this to happen.

It is difficult to know where to draw the line between knowledge and interference. Science can now achieve extraordinary results, implanting embryos into a womb, filming the progress of the foetus, and providing details of its sex and genetic make-up. These advances have grown out of the 'natural' desires to produce live, healthy babies, and to promote fertility in women who have difficulties in getting pregnant. They echo the old call of Nature for 'More babies, please!' But there is a fear that these developments may transgress natural laws, bringing too much within the domain of deliberate intervention, and promoting physical growth at the expense of the spirit. We have to weigh up the merits of medical assistance and of leaving Nature to take its course. The Great Mother is more than a blind force of Nature. She represents the responsibility for choosing life or death; she encompasses the instinctive and physical processes of gestation and birth, our knowledge of these, and our ability to manipulate them.

The process of gestation has its parallel on the psychological level. It is no mere figure of speech to say that an idea is 'born'; an idea goes through a real phase of development, from conception to birth. There is an art to recognizing when such gestation is going on, and, very often, to resisting the temptation to interfere with it. In my own case I can experience psychological feelings very similar to physical pregnancy – a vague unease, heaviness, discomfort, and a kind of dark brooding. Very often I fail to see that something is on its way to birth, and tax myself with totally useless questions as to what the matter might be. Then, at some point, the idea is ready to emerge, and, as it does so, all the tension disappears.

I do not think this experience is confined to women, but it symbolizes something of the quality of the Great Mother, and it shows how we have the ability to conceive and carry to birth on a level other than the physical. One must allow the darkness and period of waiting to be; probing and prodding can cause the embryo to abort. I have discovered that during periods of withdrawal from normal mental activity – during meditation, or while hovering on the borders of sleep, for instance – it is sometimes possible to look right into that 'teeming womb' and release its contents prematurely. There may be the germs of many good ideas there, but to allow them out and pick them over is to expose them too soon to the light of day. If one touches upon that area, it is good discipline to learn to leave well alone, and to trust that the ideas will in time emerge into consciousness. This gives them a far better chance of survival.

I have also noticed that nine months after a significant moment occurs in life, something very often happens. Taking a simple example, you might suddenly have an intimation that it is time to change direction and find a new job. You may forget about this entirely, or you may spend some time exploring possibilities in a rather inconsequential way. Then, nine months of gestation later, an opportunity crops up out of the blue, or so it seems. Turning points in relationships, too, are often mapped out in this way – a quarrel, a meeting, a reconciliation may mark the moment of 'conception'; one knows that a new phase is beginning but it does not become openly apparent until this nine-month span has past. It seems that the nine-month gestation period has a psychological as well as a physical reality in human life.

In the search for a transcendent level of knowledge, it has long been part of human endeavour to enter a symbolic womb of darkness and learn within its space. Many temples, caves, burial chambers and 'vision pits' have been constructed and used for this purpose. Here again the link between birth and death is clear, as there is often no firm distinction between 'womb' and 'tomb' in the physical construction of the chambers, or in the states that the participant is expected to experience. Initiation rites in magical sects and mystery religions often require the candidate to be shut up in a dark vault for a lengthy period, in order to die and be reborn to himself. Traces of this can be found in shamanism and Mithraism, and may well be part of the ancient Egyptian mysteries.

We can enter and be enclosed in the space of the symbolic womb and, within its oppressive, confined darkness, discover the sacred flame of spirit that is nourished there. We can also, through being placed within complete physical limitations, discover our freedom to transcend these and attain knowledge unfettered by physical constraint. Through being locked in the womb of earth, a vision of the heavens may arise.

Such visions may have a sadness ingrained in them, for they can contain the knowledge of ends as well as beginnings. The Great Mother is like a priestess sitting in the dark temple, an old, old woman, who has seen many seekers come and go, all with their own vital problems and joys. She sees the similarity of these, although each person feels unique, and she sees the likely outcomes, even though she cannot always reveal them. She will give advice compassionately, well aware that it will not always be heeded. And, through her understanding, she knows herself to be utterly and completely alone. Life passes through her domain, but she is not of it; she is beyond it.

So it is when a woman is giving birth. She is alone, no matter how much kind support she has around her. She is, at that moment, a vessel for the life that is about to emerge from her. Her sense of time may vanish, and her normal sense of self. Perceptions may change – her body can feel as vast as a mountain, and her own breathing be heard as an urgent sound coming from a different person. She is beyond time, and yet she is giving birth to time itself. At the moment of birth, her baby is the very youngest member of the human race, its star of hope and its future.

Images

Street Image

She has a couple of children with her and a third on the way. A pushchair for the smallest one, a bag of shopping, a handbag which carries more in the way of pins, wipes and sweets as bribes than it does personal possessions. She looks tired, but she has control; she pushes the younger child, answers the endless questions of the elder, and all the while senses the baby within her growing, growing.

Mythic Image

A shapeless, brooding figure, from which can emerge pain, death, life or joy. The nameless goddess of ancient cults, roughly but tenderly fashioned. The goddesses who support a myriad of lives, such as the many-breasted Artemis. The Great Mother has many forms; each of her children calls her by a different name.

Personal Image

If you have given birth, can you look back over the process and recognize how it has changed you? Did it open out a larger world for you, or confine you in a smaller one? If you have not had a child, what factors have so far prevented you? Can you still recognize the mother in yourself? For everyone, a mother image resides within us. It is created partly by our experience of our own mothers, partly by our individual nature, and partly by giving birth. It is a key to our lineage, a key to unlock the door of time.

Evolution

Youth

At some point, the physical urge to be a mother strikes home. The exact time varies enormously; some small girls are already devoted to their make-believe babies, while for others it is merely a charade they feel compelled to act out. The desire may come in adolescence, in early womanhood or even later; some claim that it never comes at all. Becoming a mother as a young woman is a powerful initiation process; life is never the same again.

Maturity

For the woman who is already a mother, the challenges are now those of coping with growing children and seeing them leave home; the challenges are always somehow different from how you have imagined them. Chances then arise to transfer that energy into another field – work, relationships, or spiritual growth. In some cultures the mother proceeds to the status of a matriarch, when she takes on the authority of mother to the whole extended family or tribe.

Old Age

The Great Mother passes through a symbolic death as she recognizes that her body can bear no more children. Through this, her love can be tempered into a compassion and understanding with which she can help and sustain others. She can be a priestess, counsellor, or wise grandmother.

Manifestations

Gifts

Birth of a child. The experience of mother love, given or received. Discovery of unexpected reserves of strength and patience. An expanded sense of time. Knowing one's own connection to the lineage of mothers, and seeing one's place in the history of women.

Trials

Loss of personal identity through looking after others. The pressure of their demands. Infertility. The death of a child, or of a mother. Physical stress of pregnancy and birth. Loss of time for oneself. The sense of a family history in which you are compelled to play a part.

Rituals and Cults

Childbirth classes; procedures and routines of maternity hospitals and midwifery. The training of midwives. Formal and informal groups of mothers centred around the welfare of children. Baby clinics, visits from health visitors, instruction in child care. Learning to counsel and guide others. Tracing family history. Participating in the rituals of one's own children – baptism, weddings, and the birth of grandchildren.

The Vision

The inevitability of birth and death, and the knowledge that love is greater than both.

The Lady of the Hearth

'I am only a poor woman and I have had no time to prepare my place properly. It is an awful mess but will you not come and sit by my fire?'

She said 'my place' as though it were some stately country house, though it was just a patch of sand scrupulously cleared of grass and thorn and scooped out into a round shallow hollow . . . On some coals drawn to the side of the neat little fire, strips of meat were laid to grill: with the subtle savour of wood smoke they spread a most provocative smell on the still air. Small and poorly appointed as her 'place' was, it had been arranged to satisfy some inner need or order . . . Standing by her place with an endearing air of domestic pride, she explained that her husband was away with the other men, spreading the meat strips on the higher thorn bushes to dry in safety. She was certain he would not be long, so again would we please sit by the fire. She stooped to brush the clean sand with her hand, as a woman might smooth a satin cushion for a guest in her drawing-room.

This meeting with a Bushman woman in Africa is described by Laurens Van der Post in his book *The Heart of the Hunter* (The Hogarth Press, 1961). The scene is touching, and, at the same time, curiously paradoxical. In one sense it is fragile, for it has the naïvety of a child's game of 'let's play house', with a little patch of ground called 'home', set out with sticks and stones. But it also has the mark of absolute reality; here, in the inhospitable desert, human family life is given meaning and security through the creation of a home base. At the heart of this home is the fire – alight for cooking, warmth, and for warding off wild animals. The family's possessions, also described by Van der Post, amount to nothing more than ostrich-egg containers, animal skins, the man's spear, bow and arrows, and the woman's 'grubbing-stick', pestle and mortar. All these, too, are arranged with order and care.

There is perhaps no better assurance of the reality of a fundamental drive than when it is seen to flourish in the most difficult and primitive circumstances. Women's efforts to create and maintain a home are found in all cultures, and it is these efforts that the Lady of the Hearth represents. Her sphere is not just a physical one for lighting a fire and tending the flame have emotional and spiritual connotations, too. Nor are all her qualities earnest ones; the 'game-playing' element in the description is greatly needed in home life. If the Lady of the Hearth principle is active in a woman's life, then it will have a pleasurable and creative quality to it. The 'playfulness' of arranging sticks and shells in the desert sand is on a par with the fun of trying out new gadgets and recipes in a modern Western kitchen. Without this sense of enjoyment and experimentation, caring for a household can become merely routine and duty. The hearth can be seen as the physical structure of the home, and the fire as the spirit that illuminates it.

This principle is not confined to any one set of living conditions, for where meaning, order and joy are generated, then any environment can be turned into a welcoming home. Although the chief focus of this chapter is the 'house' and 'home', it should also be kept in mind that this can be extended to apply to any circumstances or environment to which a woman gives structure and form. So, for instance, the interpretations can have relevance to a place of work. In essence, the Lady of the Hearth represents the way in which we choose and set out a bounded space in which to live, the fire we light at its centre, and the way we use the heat which the fire provides. We will look at each of these in turn.

Preparing the Hearth

You can walk into one house, and it feels cold and empty, walk into another and be struck by an atmosphere of friendliness and warmth. This has nothing to do with whether the house is smart or poor. The effect is usually generated by the way the home is set up, the relationship between the occupants, and the care and attention that go into maintaining the household.

Usually, much of this depends upon the woman or women who live there. Most women care intensely about the surroundings in which they live, and their sense of security is tied up with the home; their moods and personalities feed into the home and contribute to its atmosphere. There are very few women who do not find that their own happiness and the quality of their home life are vitally linked. This can be a two-way flow; a good home base can help to create contentment, and at the same time personal satisfaction in life will feed back into the home and make it a pleasant environment for others. Possibly this is why the argument as to whether it is better for a woman with young children to stay at home or go out to work goes round and round in circles. A woman who is happy in her job and hates being cooped up at home all day will bring back positive qualities to the household, but on the other hand the strains and stresses of work can also leave their mark on family life. Just as body and mind are linked, and each can affect the other, so the home and the feminine psyche are connected and will interact.

It is important to stress that this connection does not imply that there is only one way of arranging domestic life. A happy home situation does not depend upon there being a housewife in residence twenty-four hours a day, nor on a woman doing all the housework herself. We tend to think that it is a modern problem, trying to set up the best lifestyle so that the need for personal commitment to the home is balanced with other social and career activities. But, in fact, in the same way as the very ambitious career woman of today risks becoming detached from her home surroundings, so it must have been extremely difficult in the past for upper-class ladies, running homes that were full of servants, to put personal qualities into the home when all the physical work was taken on by others. The hearth itself was often fiercely guarded by a cook, and it would cause great offence if the 'lady of the house' spent any time in the kitchen, let alone tried to prepare a meal. Her role must have been curiously akin to that of the executive businesswoman today, exercising the skills of management and delegation.

There will always be varying ways in which a woman's relationship to her home is expressed, depending on the period and culture in which she lives. The challenge that many of us face today is that we have a choice – whether or not we go out to work, how much domestic machinery we use, how much we involve the rest of the family in housework, whether or not we employ someone else to do the cleaning, how many take-away meals are put on the table, and so on. Sometimes, economic factors or personal values will rigidly dictate a way of living, but for many of us there are a variety of options. We need to try to understand the principle of the relationship between a woman and her home, and to work out a pattern which suits us as individuals.

Household tasks can carry a strong emotive charge. There cannot be many women who run their homes as efficiently and as mechanically as a factory, or to the kind of strict timetables that the domestic manuals printed a generation or two ago would have us follow. These usually began with a stern injunction to rise at 6.30 a.m., first task to clear out the embers from the fire (yet another pointer to the fire as the heart of the home) and relight it. Another hour or so of heavy housework must precede breakfast, followed by a further assault on sweeping and dusting, and later, for a little light relief, pastry-making and shopping. Every hour of the day is accounted for. Such books were published mainly in the 1920s and 1930s at a time when women had to learn to take over the running of their own homes, without the help of servants any longer, but still keeping middle- and upper-class standards. The commands of these household manuals imply that the printed word was now the authority in the home, and the housewife the new model of servant obeying its dictates.

Fascinating though these books are to read, the thought of being held prisoner by such a regime, knowing exactly how each day was to be spent from now until eternity, makes me feel cold with horror. Whether their instructions were followed to the letter is, of course, a different matter; they do, however, come from an era when short cuts and convenience were frowned upon and considered synonyms for dirtiness and sloppiness. Any sense of humour, of enjoyment and playfulness is totally lacking; the implication was that a household should be tackled in exactly the same way as an institution:

When anyone is running a factory they map out every tiny detail, saying when the smallest and most important things shall be done, and by whom. It is just the same in planning a home ... Draw up a plan labelled 'Weekly Jobs', and write down under each day its special task ... Then draw up a chart marked 'Daily Jobs', and write down in detail each thing, beginning, 'Put on the kettle, light fire and clear out ashes,' and so on.

(*Every Woman's Enquire Within*, c. 1930)

I suppose this set of instructions at least offers you the liberty of constructing your own timetable. In a sense, when running a household becomes a drudgery, then it is like sitting by a cold, empty hearth with no fire. The vital spirit of the Lady of the Hearth is missing.

Perhaps the mother–daughter relationship is also significant in respect of whether the Lady enters your life easily, or only after a long struggle. When a mother instils in her daughter a strong sense of obligation towards the house, to keeping it clean, tidy, impeccably dusted, the daughter in her turn may find herself either an unhappy slave to these expectations, or else determinedly anarchic in her own home. The reverse can also be true; where a mother has been a haphazard housekeeper her daughter may either exercise rigid control or be totally at sea in the house. It can take a long time for a woman to rid herself of the automatic assumptions that she has absorbed about home-making, and learn to fashion an approach which suits her and her family.

We might speculate that we need to teach the next generation the principles of establishing the Lady of the Hearth, the ways in which an environment can be made a happy, welcoming place. Not the specific details, because domestic life is changing so radically from decade to decade: its structure is also strongly influenced by patterns of child care and external work. The Lady of the Hearth may help us to see what is essential, rather than ephemeral: a place to call one's own, a heart within it, a sense of order, and a sense of fun to balance it.

These are the constants, not the timetables. How they are put into practice will vary, not only because of changing external circumstances, but also because our own state fluctuates, and we adapt our domestic lives to some degree to our changing levels of energy and mood. It is often the case that when all is going well in life, tackling a heavy job can seem a treat, whereas in times of stress a dirty footprint on a new-washed floor is the last straw. Sometimes, of course, it can work the other way round; I recall a woman, going through a difficult time with her husband, returning after a few days' holiday to find that he had swept and cleaned the house from top to bottom. She sat down on her suitcases and howled, feeling that he had swept the last traces of her personality out in the dustpan too.

As I have already suggested, unless care is taken, work in the house can become a focus for negative emotions. Feelings of being a martyr to the vacuum cleaner, or of struggling to live up to impossible standards of cleanliness, can take the pleasure out of time spent in the home. The choices we make as to what jobs we do, and how often we do them, are not always in our own best interests. If there is the opportunity to buy a dishwasher, for instance, why refuse? Maybe because the routine of washing-up is basically enjoyable – hot water and clean plates at the end of it. Some tasks help to ground us, give us time to think and allow us to feel more in touch with the domestic cycle. But maybe the offer is refused because the kitchen sink has been enthroned as the living nerve-centre of the home, and to abandon it is to lose the right to be considered worthy and hard-working; she who washes the dishes puts everybody else under an obligation. In that case, the refusal is a loaded one and perpetuates an emotional interaction of dubious value.

In setting up a home routine, we can in fact forgo the opportunity to make intelligent choices by responding to certain kinds of pressure. By intelligent, I do not mean intellectual, but based on a wise consideration of our emotional and physical needs, and those of other members of the household. We have the power to create a welcoming, healthy space for living which will nurture others as well as ourselves. We have the ability to colour it through our personalities, and shape it according to our imagination. This requires personal understanding of each individual situation, not a blind response to ideals and opinions.

Setting up a 'hearth' corresponds to setting up a home. To make a hearth, a space has to be defined and, to some extent, separated from its surroundings, with stone, fire guards and so on – just as a house has walls and boundary fences. The hearth has to be made of materials which will withstand heat and provide the right structure for the particular fuel to burn in. Here there is a similarity with the way in which a home is set up to cope with the needs and activities of its occupants, who may be compared with the living fire on the hearth! (The active heat of small children, for instance, is best contained in a house of robust furnishings rather than delicate antiques!) Lastly, the hearth has to be tended, constantly supplied with fuel, and this can be likened to the need for the home to be paid ongoing care and attention, the absence of which will be felt as a cold and empty atmosphere.

Ritual has a place in domestic activity. Ritual is in some ways akin to routine, the process of regularizing actions. However, whereas routine can become mechanical, ritual itself is always intended as a conscious act. Ritual is an action taken on the physical level, which is intended to have effects at other levels – emotional, mental, spiritual, or all of these. It is a linking of the intangible with the tangible, which can only come about through conscious intention. Ritual action is prescribed, ordered and deliberate. It is often symbolic, or makes use of symbols, since a symbol is a visible form of a quality or ideal. The connection between rituals of the hearth and fire and the work of priestesses in a temple is a very ancient one. There are records of rites which involved tending the sacred flame in a religious context, and of other customs which bestowed religious significance on the domestic fire. In rural Ireland, rituals have been observed for 'smooring the fire', preserving the household fire overnight by making the sign of the cross in the ashes and calling upon the spirit of the Virgin Mary to keep the embers alive until morning. Tending the hearth can remind a woman of the sacred mysteries that she serves, and can, in effect, turn a housewife into a priestess.

This is stepping ahead to the next consideration of the Lady of the Hearth as she who lights and tends the fire. Ritual might properly be considered a stage between this present section, on preparing the hearth, and the next, on lighting the fire, for it can be a means of enlivening a situation and of allowing positive energies to flow into the structure prepared. There are many traces of ritual in ordinary household life, and perhaps these could be made more use of, and new ones established. The borderline between ritual and custom is a little blurred; custom could be said to be a form of ritual that has lost many of its magical or religious overtones, but still retains some of the original intent to transform. With a little thought, we can find plenty of such customs/rituals in the home. Take, for instance, the English Sunday lunch. It conjures up a vision of a large, appetizing meal, around which the whole family gathers, to share food and conversation in an especially leisurely way. The intention is that the members of the household should have an opportunity to communicate with each other, to sense their unity as a family, and to enjoy time set aside from the normal rush of daily life. This is a collective ritual in which everyone plays a part. There may, of course, be some discrepancy between the ideal and the reality, and we may better understand the positive potential of the custom by remembering how easily it can be spoilt if something goes wrong. A surly teenager can sour the occasion by sulking, and the burning of the joint gathers tragic overtones.

Bringing a ritual element into the home implies doing something over and above what is physically necessary. For example, all that is physically necessary as regards food is to make sure that everyone has enough of the right sort. But our mealtime patterns develop social implications too; special meals have particular significance for the family, and perhaps some, such as Christmas dinner, may have religious meaning. At the other end of the scale, a small and humble task can sometimes be given ritual status by attending to it with real attention and care. On the occasions when I have tried this, I have found that I enjoy admiring what I have done much more than usual – the finished job seems to have a glow, which lasts longer than one would expect.

Physical ordering can create order also at the psychological and personal level. Spring-cleaning, repainting and clearing out cupboards can all be good ways of dispelling any unpleasant or heavy atmosphere that has built up in the home. It has also been said that such activities can help to raise the general level of energy of members of the household, the depletion of which may often show itself as a succession of minor illnesses. If we look at the ways in which we handle daily tasks, we shall probably find a strong ritual element there, and that a fair proportion of the setting-to-rights we do is as much for our personal well-being as from physical necessity.

Lighting and Tending the Fire

When the hearth is prepared, the fire can be lit. This does not happen so often nowadays in literal terms, central heating and portable fires have taken care of that. I made the discovery, on moving to a country home with large, temperamental wood-burning stoves, that I was woefully ill-educated in the lighting and management of fires. My poetic image of the Lady of the Hearth was grounded sharply on one particular occasion when, suffering from raging flu, and having to cope with the demands of two small children in a freezing house, I struggled over and over again to make the wood catch fire. There is more skill to this than many people realize.

A Lady of the Hearth who does not personally oversee her fire can be heading for trouble, and the men around may not be much use either. This moral is highlighted by an episode from my own family annals which occurred when we were visiting my in-laws in Scotland. On the first evening we had a lively dinner for the temporary extended family, during which much enthusiastic talking and a fair amount of equally enthusiastic drinking took place. In the sitting room next door a log fire burned. My mother-in-law, remembering that it was a while since she had tended it, told my son with an expansive wave of her hand to 'go and pile logs on'. He cheerfully did as he was told; taking her command literally he heaped as many logs on as the large fireplace would take. Some time later we were alerted by a smell of burning, and rushed out to find the chimney on fire.

At this point, the men, fancying their prowess in an emergency, insisted on taking over the action and promised a speedy end to the conflagration by pinning an old piece of carpet across the fireplace. This, they assured us, would cut out the air and so stop the flames. We were doubtful. It wasn't long, of course, before the superb 'draught excluder' thus created burst into a spectacular display of flames, which shot out across the room.

Now it was the women's turn again; while the men debated the finer points of why the device had failed, we fetched buckets of water and old blankets and quickly put out the fire. Fortunately there was little damage, so I can remember the event with hilarity. Looking after a fire does require a modicum of attention and responsibility.

The lighting and keeping of the hearth fire have always been given significance in human culture; the Greeks named their goddess of the hearth Hestia, later to be replaced by the Roman Vesta, whose handmaidens were the famous Vestal Virgins.

In a religious context, the lighting of the fire may become the lighting of lamps or candles. On Friday nights in Jewish households, the lady of the house performs the sacred ritual of lighting two candles and requesting through prayer that the presence of the Lord should bless the gathered family. Through this ceremony, the Sabbath is begun; the woman invites the divine spirit into the home.

Lighting the fire sets in motion a new sequence of action. The fuel, dormant and immobile, will now be transformed into heat and light and can never again resume its former state. If the ritual of lighting the flame is done consciously, it can have an especially powerful effect; the moment marks a change-point, the entry into a new state. Once, in an American girls' school, I watched a prize-giving ceremony in which candles were lit one by one, accompanied by spoken declarations such as: 'I light the lamp of scholarship'. A teenager myself at the time, I found the occasion awkward and somewhat embarrassing, as I suspect some of the pupils did. It did not accord at all with the normal context of school life. But probably for this very reason, I have not forgotten it and I doubt if the participants have either. It marked the occasion in a special way. The conscious intent, and the time taken to perform an action that had clear symbolic content, drew our attention and created an out-of-the ordinary impression. Such a description might sound high-flown for a small, transitory occasion. However, whether a small spark is struck or a blazing fire lit, the flame is the same. A minor act of dedication and commitment, which the lighting of the flame represents, may initiate an effect just as a major one can.

For the individual woman, the taking of a new step can be the moment at which her own nature affirms itself. The affirmation will be all the stronger if she acts with self-knowledge and compassion, and even with a certain sense of detachment. There must be a quietness and a space surrounding the act for it to be fully effective. To act in the heat of passion is to perpetuate a present state, not to initiate a new one; for something new to come in, space has to be made. Words flung out in temper, for instance, do not carry lasting conviction although they may wound at the time, whereas a calm statement, arising from inner knowledge, is likely to come from the centre of one's being and to hold fast. This is often how relationships are truly forged and broken; through being centred, it is easier to know one's own mind, and to bring a quiet force of will into play which is more effective than any histrionic display. The words of marriage ceremonies are in fact usually spoken in just such a low-key but deliberate manner.

Once the fire is lit, it has to be kept going and refuelled as necessary. The first aspect that presents itself is one of sheer hard slog! On the literal level, I learnt this at first hand with our notorious stoves. They consumed a prodigious amount of fuel, logs which had to be carted in by the barrow-load, stacked to dry, and fed frequently into the ravenous, red-hot maw of the burner. Any kind of open fire needs a considerable volume of fuel to keep it alight. There is some leeway as to when you choose to bring in the next hod of coal and restoke your boiler, but not a lot; leave it too long and the fire goes out, and you must start all over again. Tending the fire is like tending relationships, children, and household tasks. Considerable regular input is required and this can become extremely repetitive, even boring. This is easily seen in the mundane example of housework, which cannot be done by making sporadic once-off assaults on it, but needs constant attention. It is not always so obvious in relationships, where we often expect the bright flames of love to burn out of their own purity and spontaneity, but they too need refuelling in what may be quite prosaic ways. There is an art to the task; it is possible, otherwise, to put out the fire by smothering it with too much fuel, or even to poke it up too hard so that the last embers blaze up and the fire dies.

The second way of considering the tending of the fire is to compare it to the feminine ability to create and sustain atmosphere. Keeping a steady blaze is akin to the way in which women generate and maintain emotional energy. For instance, which of us has not prolonged an atmosphere of hostility by keeping the coals smouldering within? It has more staying power than a quick outburst of rage. We can evoke particular qualities of feeling as we choose, drawing from our own emotional resources. A mother with small children, for example, may need to generate qualities of reassurance, or calmness, or affection, according to the needs of the moment. In a curious way, women are probably more prone than men to changes of mood, but are more able to manipulate them. An eminent psychologist has remarked that a man in a mood is almost as if in the grip of a small psychosis, and can find himself helpless in the face of it, unless he has trained himself not to identify with it too strongly. A woman, on the other hand, is used to moods and can often change them at will, as if stepping into a new outfit of clothes (Robert A. Johnson, *He – Understanding Masculine Psychology*).

Mood and emotion are not entirely the same psychological phenomenon, as emotion is capable of greater refinement and of putting a person in touch with more profound experience. Moods and feelings are perhaps more closely connected, and it is from her 'repertoire' of feelings that a woman can choose, in order to project particular qualities to colour her environment. She can, if she so wishes, create a warm and friendly atmosphere in her home, or a cool artistic quality. A household that feels 'neutral' or empty may indicate that the woman who lives there is cut off from her own emotions. The same cannot so readily be said of a man, who does not necessarily imprint his surroundings with personal feelings. Women have a natural link between the psyche and the physical, of which they can make valuable use.

Enjoying the Fire

With the hearth swept, and the fire lit and stoked, hospitality can be extended. Food can be cooked, stories exchanged, and time left for gazing silently into the flames, watching the dancing shapes at the heart of the fire. The fire is a focus for communication and for vision; its heat serves physical needs and its flames give inspiration for the mind. The Lady of the Hearth is a reminder of how the mundane, prosaic side of life is intimately connected to that which is highest and freest in us. All the preparatory work can lead to sheer enjoyment of the fire.

The message brought by the Lady of the Hearth is that we may allow ourselves time and space to enjoy the fruits of the work – for this, too, is part of the cycle. It is all too easy to spend a back-breaking couple of hours weeding the garden and never take ten minutes to sit and look at the flowers. The demands of children can be so insistent that a mother never uses the odd quiet moment to sit down with them and enjoy their company; the temptation is always to seek out the next task.

Every woman can make time in her life to pause, reflect and enjoy, if she will allow herself to do so. This also gives a chance for creative ideas to arise. Women, I think, have to be canny in creating these opportunities for themselves, since they do not, on the whole, lead such compartmentalized lives as men, with separate times for 'work' and 'play'. Hence there is a need to seek out opportunities for creativity in the general fabric of daily life. 'Creative' is an over-used word nowadays, not easy to define: The 'taste' of creative effort is sometimes a sense of at-oneness with the project, as though you and your task are sharing the same living energy. Creativity is not restricted to painting magnificent pictures. It can be found in baking a cake, pruning a tree, or holding a children's party. Every individual has to find her way of tapping and using her creative resources, whether her daily environment is a home or an office.

The fire of the Lady of the Hearth also symbolizes the way in which we can reach back to the past and forward to the future. The fire has long been a focus for the telling of stories, and for the stimulation of inner vision. Often, the history of a tribe has been perpetuated as the grandmothers of the village tell the old tales yet again around the evening fire. Even today, children retain vivid impressions from the stories told to them by their mothers and grandmothers about their own childhoods 'long ago'. Story-telling can keep alive the sense of continuity of family or tribal life. Stories can teach, entertain, and entrance, and women have long had a reputation for creating an atmosphere which keeps the listener spellbound. Think of the princess in *The Arabian Nights*, for instance, who distracted the king from his evil intentions for one thousand and one nights, by telling him a different story every night. Story-telling is considered a part of a woman's magical repertoire – a device she can use to affect the listener, melting his heart, distracting him or binding him to her as the occasion demands.

Perhaps this has receded a little into the background in modern life, especially in a literate society with easy recourse to television, books and newspapers. But work that has been done with story-telling in women's groups shows that it can be tremendously enjoyable, and bring out a range of expression and imaginative ideas in every participant. It would be nice if some way could be found of keeping this tradition alive in modern society.

Tales are usually of the past, but they can be of the future too. The leaping flame of the fire can call to mind strange images, which seem to be beyond the boundaries of normal knowledge. Such images may be the food which fuels paintings and stories, or they may seem to be glimpses into an unknown world, one that we have not yet met. Divining the future, where such ability exists, is not solely of the feminine province, but is possibly more readily accessible to women. To divine requires a willingness to let go of 'rational' concepts, and to allow intuition and imagination to be the communicators of information. It may also be that women have a greater need of seeing some of the qualities of the future. We are conservers and preservers, maintaining homes and relationships, and we do not always welcome change. The 'hearths' of the future may be very different, as technology transforms our homes and space travel whisks human beings away to alien environments. Granting ourselves the time to speculate and dream of a world to come gives us a chance to prepare for and adapt to a future way of life.

Images

Street Image

She's out enjoying a Saturday shopping trip – there are people coming to dinner tonight, and when she's stocked up on the basic necessities, she'll choose some extra delights from the delicatessen. If time permits, she'll be pondering some new colour schemes for a room that she wants to redecorate. She seems to bump into quite a few people that she knows, exchanges greetings, bits of news, and invites one or two to visit. She doesn't linger too long, for there are preparations to be made at home.

Mythic Image

The Lady of the Hearth can be invoked when you move into a new home. If the atmosphere is welcoming, then her presence is already there; but take care that you put a little something back during your time in the house, because the saddest thing of all is to let that warmth dwindle away over the years. If you need to call upon her, then do it as you decorate, arrange the furniture and set the spaces for living. Remember that she responds to laughter, and lightness and warmth, her attributes.

Personal Image

Can you walk into your home or work-space and see it with new eyes? If you were seeing it for the first time, what impressions would you receive? What does it smell like? What sort of feeling will you associate with it when it is only a memory from the past? Consider how you went about setting it up, and whether it was a trial or a delight, or a mixture of the two. Are there any changes you would like to make now? The Lady of the Hearth in you is that which chooses a space, orders it, and imprints it with your personality.

Evolution

Youth

Small girls can be found playing at 'house', disconcerting their feminist mothers. The teenage girl may guard her space jealously; if she has the chance she will make it uniquely hers, experimenting with posters, plants, and colours. Her room becomes a refuge for her and her close friends. The young woman feels curiously as though she is only playing at house once more when she goes into the first flat or home that she can truly call her own. Is she really free to be as tidy or untidy as she pleases? Who shall she invite round first? Buying two wooden spoons can be more fun at this time than purchasing an expensive set of china in later years.

Maturity

Now the woman has established her pattern and may not pay much conscious attention to her surroundings, if they serve her needs well. She knows the kinds of places she likes to work, sleep and eat in, and will instinctively seek out the right type of office, hotel, or restaurant. The rules and regulations of her domain are established, and woe betide members of the household who break them.

Old Age

Tolerance creeps back in. A layer of dust seems less important now that the years are numbered. Children who visit may absorb a magical sense of bygone years in a home which is furnished and run in the style of fifty years ago. In old age, the teller of tales comes to the fore, the external pace dies down, the internal clock ticks to a steadier pulse. There is space for a story to unfold.

Manifestations

Gifts

Good company. Gift of creating a pleasant environment with minimal resources. A sense of atmosphere and place. A love of history. Visions of the future. A gift of story-telling. Receiving hospitality.

Trials

Poverty and poor housing conditions. Being compelled to live in accommodation not of one's own choosing. Being forced to uproot from a place one loves and has made one's own. Lack of a permanent base. Living communally against one's will, having no space of one's own. Pressure of time, leaving no space for relaxation and contemplation.

Rituals and Cults

Moving house; preliminary and formal procedures, packing, re-decorating etc. Ceremonies of fire-lighting and tending. The rites of entertaining and offering hospitality. Gatherings for story-telling and for recalling the past. Divination through visionary means.

The Vision

The sacred gift of fire; the conditions necessary for striking it and maintaining it.

7

The Queen of the Earth

The Making of a Queen

A queen is not born as such: she generally starts life as a princess. When she first ascends to the throne, her personal nature is subordinated to the role that she has taken on. Only later does this queen make her mark as an individual, so she will be remembered by her character and deeds. She has moved from small letter queen, to capital letter Queen, with her own name attached. 'A queen' conjures up a generalized set of associations. 'An English Queen' or 'A Russian Empress' paints a more specific picture. But Queen Victoria, or Catherine the Great, are complete portraits, strongly differentiated identities who have imprinted their personalities on history like a seal on a roll of parchment.

The Queen of the Earth represents the complete process of this development. She is at once the Princess, the enthroned Queen and the differentiated individual Queen. As her title, 'of the Earth', implies, she is bound up with cycles of growth, and their seed, blossom and fruit, with knowledge of the seasons, and with knowledge of the nature of the earth itself, of the hidden properties of the soil and of what lies beneath the surface of the ground. In feminine terms the life cycle of the Queen of the Earth is linked to sexuality, and can be divided into three phases: the 'innocent', the 'awoken', and the 'individualized'. These phases could be construed as following chronologically in a woman's life. However, as I shall try to convey, these apparently separate stages are also three elements of sexuality which can coexist in a grown woman. In one sense, the literal, physical unfolding of girl into woman follows each of these three stages in turn, but, in another, more complete sense, all three of these aspects of the Queen of the Earth can be present in adult life. Our earth is immersed in a cycle of seasons, as it turns on its axis, and so we too find ourselves involved in new beginnings and cycles of growth. We can come back over and over again to an intense awareness of any of the three stages, although each time our standpoint may be a little different.

It will be helpful to keep this in mind as we investigate the realm of the Queen of the Earth. I will describe the three sides of her nature – the Princess, the Queen and the named Queen – in their obvious order; this order can be taken to reflect the stages that a woman reaches at successive points in her life; but the three aspects may also correspond to cycles of inner growth which can be initiated at any age. They may relate to sexual, emotional or spiritual growth; again, it is unwise to make assumptions that development follows a 'natural' course, first of the body, then of the psyche and lastly of the spirit. A new understanding of spiritual matters, for instance, can bring increased knowledge of sexual power, too.

The Princess – Happy and Free

The Greek goddess Artemis, in one legend, begged her father never to make her marry. It was not because she was averse to men – indeed some of the myths relate that she had many love affairs – but because the freedom she enjoyed would be shattered by marriage. She roamed the hills and forests of Arcadia, with her companions; she was free to run, hunt, bathe and wander as she pleased. She was at one with the wildness of nature and the inclination of her own spirit.

Most girlhoods have this quality of freedom embedded in them. It is perhaps related particularly to the pre-adolescent stage, between the ages of about 7 and 12. At this time the body is lithe and nimble and many girls enjoy sports, especially athletics and horse-riding. They may take some care of their appearance, but only as a game; there is not the self-consciousness that comes with adolescence, but on the other hand there is a pleasure in one's own company and a growing sense of independence. When happiness is present, it has a purity. This kind of delight in being alive is not usually triggered by praise from someone else, or by personal achievements. It can be lit up by simple perceptions – the smell of lunch cooking, the sight of primroses growing in the moss, or the feel of the wind on one's cheeks. Later, the senses can be veiled by all kinds of considerations, moods and thoughts. We cease to take things for what they are; the adolescent may be moved by nature, but probably wants to write a highly emotional poem about it.

The 'young' Queen of the Earth symbolizes our immediate responses to the world around us. Impressions gained through the senses at this stage are direct; sexuality is like sap running through a growing tree; it seeks no conscious counterpart outside itself. During this phase of girlhood we may form strong and lasting attachments to the particular environments and qualities that stimulate such moments, moments when we feel complete and happy and life holds no complications. In later years we may long to get back to country life and find those primroses again, or perhaps to live in a cosy terraced house like the one where we had tea each week with a favourite aunt. The sense of being a 'child of Nature' can blossom whether one's childhood is spent in the city or in the country. A medieval poem, 'The Maiden lay in the Wilds', touches most poignantly upon this half-forgotten longing. Shortened, it reads:

> Maiden in the moor lay . . . Seven night full . . .
>   Seven nights full and a day.
> Well was her meat. What was her meat?
> The primrose and the violet.
> Well was her drink. What was her drink?
> . . . The cold water of the well-spring.
> Well was her bower. What was her bower?
> . . . The red rose and the lily flower.
>
> (Anonymous, 14th century)

The Princess is free so far from duties and responsibilities. The earth is her playground, its creatures her companions. Sexuality exists, but is no cause for concern; although the young girl may present a fetching picture to others, she is generally unaware of it, and, indeed, if she does come to realize it, she may lose that innocent beauty which made her so attractive. It is as if her attention is not directed towards herself; the connection between her and her surroundings is open, and a play of joyful interaction continues between them.

Later, we may sense that this quality is still alive somewhere within us. We seek ways of bringing it out again – to be natural, spontaneous, uninhibited. In recent years there has been a growing interest in what the term 'virgin' can really be taken to imply, and the suggestion has been made that it denotes, in fact, the woman who is complete unto herself, at one with herself. She may engage in sexual activity, and be a mother, but she is one in her essence, not half of someone else. So, as well as representing an early stage of girlhood, the term can define a part of our being which we feel is 'untouched'. It can also relate to a desire for self-fulfilment and independence. After long involvement with child rearing, or with a close, dependent partnership, a woman may conceive a desire for rediscovering her own company and refashioning her life.

The film *Shirley Valentine* takes the working-class heroine from a dreary life of housework and husband to an exotic Greek island where she has a romantic affair with a local restaurateur. He, it turns out, picks a woman a week off the incoming boat, but she is not perturbed when she discovers this, because, she says, the love affair has been chiefly with herself. She has re-found the freedom and the person that she lost during adolescence; Artemis is still free to roam the hills. This is a light-hearted film, but it is interesting that it has had a large following from a female audience, while the male sector has paid it only scant and grudging attention.

I am not suggesting that independence is the only desirable goal for womanhood. In fact, in the context of the film it was implied that Shirley Valentine would start on a new cycle, perhaps entering back into a different and better relationship with her husband. The Queen of the Earth implies that there are three ways of existing; we can move through them in sequence; we can possess them all simultaneously, or we can emphasize one at the expense of the others. Thinking about the 'Princess' phase, there are certainly women who seem to have remained 'untouched', even though they have been married and had children. There are others who have chosen to revert to that state when their children have grown up, especially if their marriages have ended, and it is hard to remember that they have ever been part of a family unit.

A general desire to recapture the 'happy Artemis' can be seen in trends in fashion and living. Every now and then, clothes revert to a careless naïvety, such as in the late 1960s' hippie era, when flowers, natural fabrics, smocks, beads, sandals and long hair all recalled the natural innocence of the daisy field, or the game of dressing up as Maid Marian in the forest. Trends arise where it is seen as desirable to 'get back to nature', dropping undue artificiality in manners, moving to the country, growing vegetables, and generally trying to live in tune with natural surroundings. Women play a very large part in such a trend; generally, their timetable is more flexible and they are able to choose whether energy should be diverted into activities which work with raw materials such as baking bread, dyeing cloth, growing herbs and gathering wild fruit. In other words, in Western society, we no longer normally do such things for economic reasons, for reasons of sheer survival. Women have choice over their life-style, and, where they are in charge of running a household, can opt for as little or as much 'nature' and manual involvement as they wish.

Keeping a slot in one's life for this can be a way of keeping contact with the youthful earth goddess. Or such a contact may be fostered by carrying on with one of those early interests, a sport or a hobby. It may spring into life with laughter, and spontaneous enjoyment, such as when women get together simply for the pleasure of it, discovering a freedom and a delight in each other's company that is often lacking amid the more serious duties of adult life.

Taking Power

The Queen of the Earth is crowned as she awakens to her powers and uses them. Let us consider this through imaginative means first. Picture a scene which may have happened many hundreds of years ago:

It is dark, and suffocatingly hot. You, a young woman, are with a throng of other women, enclosed in a space which may be a thick-walled hut, or a cave – you cannot tell. The ground beneath your naked feet is of beaten earth. It is warm to the touch, and on its smooth surface there is the gritty, whiskery feeling of corn. As you roll your foot, you can feel the prickly ears of corn and the smoother, nuttier grains that have burst out of their husks. There is noise – loud, chaotic, with much laughter and the odd strange cry, like that of a female animal calling in the night. You join with the others, stamping and kicking the sprinkled corn. You slither and roll, linking arms with the others so that you do not fall. The shouts come louder now, then unify, turning into a sort of chant, and the stamping develops into the rhythm of a dance. The freed grains of corn begin to form into little mounds. Bodies are hot and sweaty; you are all naked. You smell this pungent, spiced odour that you will remember for the rest of your life. Now you push and pull each other, too, as the rhythm of the dance builds, and the chants become shrieks – until there is one loud cry which seems to burst out from all of you at once.

Many months later, you are taken out to the fields and there see the tender green shoots of corn sprouting up from the grains which you threshed. This is the turning-point from dark to light, from seed to harvest. You are shown it so that you may recognize the beginnings of life, and remember what you poured into it in the dark.

This is not a historical account, but an imaginative one. We do know that there is a long association between harvest and the feminine. In the Eleusinian Mysteries of ancient Greece, whose content still remains largely a mystery today, Demeter, the corn goddess, was a presiding deity.

In survivals of British harvest customs, practised well into the last century, the feminine element was predominant, for the last sheaf of corn to be cut in the field was known as 'The Neck', and was thought to embody the female Corn Spirit. 'The Neck' was fashioned into a 'corn dolly', which might be known as either the 'Maiden' or the 'Old Woman'. Corn, in the form of wheat and barley, was the earliest crop grown by mankind, and has remained one of the most important. It is the basis of bread, a staple food; it can be stored to last through the barren months of winter, and a portion of it can be replanted to produce the next summer's harvest. Harvest stands as a symbol of feminine sexuality at a general, collective level. Links made between sex and threshing of corn are also common currency. Various folk songs relate lusty encounters while the corn is being threshed or milled. The imaginative account above is obviously sexual, in terms of the energy evoked, and the climactic quality reached through the pounding and pushing of corn and bodies. A collective sexuality is thus generated and released into the work on hand. Traditionally, there has been a connection between the arousal of sexual energy and involvement in the natural world; either it has become dormant, or else it only emerges in less obvious ways in today's society. In previous centuries, licensed collective sexuality was, for instance, tied into the passing seasons. In the spring, English youth flocked to the woods on the eve of May Day (it was approximately two weeks later then than it is now, due to calendar changes, so the weather might have been warmer) and spent the night there, enjoying each other in the full sense of the word, and bringing home boughs of the mayflower in triumph the following morning. Thus the Queen comes into her power, and the fullness of sexuality is acknowledged and experienced.

We do not have intense harvest or nature rituals in this part of the world today, nor do we have socially accepted initiation rites celebrating the passage of young girls into womanhood. There is, however, a kind of shared sense of sexuality which most girls enter in their teenage years. When I went to a girls' secondary school, at the age of 11, we were told to change together for our first gym lesson. The cloakroom became a mass of wriggling bodies, as we contorted ourselves in an attempt to preserve our modesty. The games mistress swept in, clapped her hands and called out: 'Nothing to be ashamed of. We're all girls together!' (She was ever thus remembered!) There was some embarrassment and giggling, but we did as we were told, and within the week were stripping off in front of each other and thinking nothing of it.

If girls have the chance to live together, or coexist, for at least part of the time, they can create an atmosphere of trust and confidence, in which sexual development can be compared and talked about. Sex comes extremely high on the agenda, however much a well-washed class of thirteen-year-olds seems to be immersed in the geography of Sri Lanka. There is speculation, gossip, the telling of anecdotes, and probably a fair amount of boasting and lying, too. It is not always cosy, because there can be pockets of ignorance and fear, especially the fear of being too different from anyone else. But there is a collectivity to which a girl can relate. There is mutual influence, too, so that the level of sexual experiment for an individual often relates to what is acceptable in the peer group. A girl may be cautious or reckless according to her individual nature, but it is almost bound to bear some relation to the group 'norm'.

At the moment, there is a lack of ritual structure, or 'rites of passage', in our society. The views of parents, as well as individual religious beliefs, have some influence on the development of sexuality in young women, but there is no generally accepted mode for this. Sex education gives technical knowledge, but although teachers may be most conscientious about trying to incorporate the emotional aspects of sexual relationships into the syllabus, that is not the same as a moral, magical or religious approach which places sexuality into a larger world view. I think that this is a task facing us in the future. Sexuality is not just a list of dos and don'ts. It relates to psychic energies, it confers power and responsibility, and brings an intensity into many types of human contact. Sexual energy is recognized in many cultures as being part of the whole understanding of human potential. In certain systems – whether, for instance, in sexual 'Tantric' yogic practices, or, at the other extreme, in the celibacy of Christian monastic life – sexual energy is viewed as a precious power to be channelled and controlled, and which can lead to spiritual ecstasy.

Entry into full sexuality for a young woman can be both frightening and exciting. There can be points in life, too, where a mature woman 'wakes up' to her sexual powers, and this is not necessarily a comfortable experience. She has a choice; she can either hold back these powers, keeping the horizons as narrow as they were before, or use them. If she opts for the latter, then further choices await her, since she can follow the obvious course and strike up new sexual relationships, or she can try to use her sexuality as a kind of basic fuel for life. Sexual energy can deepen friendships, and spark off creativity.

The Queen of the Earth, ascending her throne, is a symbol of the living beauty of the earth, of the plants and creatures and contours of the landscape. This can be perceived imaginatively; if you look out of a train window you may see the hills as the velvet-covered curves of a body, the fields as patchwork robes, crafted in rich materials, and the spring leaves on a tree as fine hair. There are many beautiful poems and myths likening women to the blossoms and fruits of nature. In mystical vein, the female beloved in the Song of Solomon announces:

I am the rose of Sharon, and the lily of the valleys.
As the lily among thorns, so is my love among the daughters.

(Chapter 2, verses 1, 2)

and her lover describes her thus:

Thy belly is like an heap of wheat set about with lilies.
Thy two breasts are like two young roes that are twins . . .
This thy stature is like to a palm tree, and thy breasts to clusters of grapes.

(Chapter 6, verses 2, 3, 7)

In British custom, the prettiest local girl (but not, originally, a child) was chosen as the May Queen in a ceremony that celebrated the new flowering of the spring, this being the civilized day custom, rather than the night custom of sexual license described above.

The sexuality embodied by the Queen of the Earth as she takes power has in it both the pulsating, hot drive of physical desire and the beautiful flowering that comes as she responds to the sexual energy, refines it, and is transformed by it. Both the 'earthiness' and the 'floweriness' are needed in the full unfolding of sexuality. The Corn Goddess and the May Queen represent these two qualities. The Corn Goddess has a wild, passionate, even savage spirit that, traditionally, was considered dangerous to encounter. The May Queen, symbolized by the delicate white foam of spring blossom, is a safer, more gracious, delightful figure.

They are both a celebration of the earth, its mysteries, and women's connection with these. It should not be too difficult to find aspects of each in ourselves, and also to see that one of them carried to excess without the balancing force of the other would be unsatisfactory. A Corn Goddess let loose becomes rapacious, violent, unmanageable. A May Queen allowed to reign all year round becomes vain, sentimental and self-indulgent.

Both elements are intricately combined in a twelfth-century poem written in praise of the Virgin Mary, by Abbess Hildegard of Bingen. The term 'Virgin' should not be taken as applying only to the 'Princess' or virgin stage of the Queen of the Earth as described here, for the full significance of the Virgin Mary is as a woman who retained her purity at the same time as manifesting her fertility in giving birth to the divine son. She is purity and passion combined.

The poem is set to plainsong, and an extract in translation reads:

O VIRIDISSIMA VIRGA

Hail, o greenest branch . . .
For the beautiful flower sprang from you . . .
Whence the skies bestowed dew upon the pasture,

and all the Earth was made joyful
because her womb
brought forth corn . . .
Then there was harvest ready for Man
and a great rejoicing of banqueters,
whence, o sweet Virgin,
no joy is lacking in you.

(From a selection of Hildegard's sequences and hymns, edited by
Christopher Page, Antico Church Music, 1983)

The Named Queen – the Garden of the Queen of Hearts

A large rose-tree stood near the entrance of the garden: the roses
growing on it were white, but there were three gardeners at it, busily
painting them red. Alice thought this a very curious thing, and she
went nearer to watch them, and just as she came up to them she heard
one of them say, 'Look out now, Five! Don't go splashing paint over me
like that!' . . .

'Would you tell me, please,' said Alice, a little timidly, 'why you are
painting those roses?'

Five and Seven said nothing, but looked at Two. Two began, in a low
voice, 'Why, the fact is, you see, Miss, this here ought to have been a
red rose-tree, and we put a white one in by mistake, and if the Queen
was to find out, we should all have our heads cut off, you know . . .'

(Lewis Carroll, *Alice's Adventures in Wonderland*, 1865)

A Queen established in her reign can be capricious. It is accepted
that she be wilful, and even eccentric, as long as she carries out
her royal duties and keeps her dignity in public. Alice's Queen of
Hearts cries 'Off with their heads!' on impulse, and plays croquet
with flamingos for mallets and hedgehogs for balls. This dream
queen is certainly crazier than most real-life ones, but nevertheless those queens who leave their mark in history are those who
rule with individuality. Their own tastes become part of their
image, whether these revolve around a love of horses, dancing,
music or men. They become symbols of an era, and their own
personal style and the fashions of the era entwine. We speak of
'Victorian' and 'Queen Anne' styles; we associate clothes, or
architecture, or social values with them. The word 'Elizabethan'

conjures up associations of a whole era – richly coloured dress, beautiful music, exquisite paintings and poetry.

The Queen of the Earth is united with her land; her character can shape the landscape and give it individuality. She draws life from the earth and gives it back again in her own manner. There is mutual feeding and reinforcing, just as a good Queen in real life can strengthen her country, unite its people, and be supported by it. To do this, she must understand its nature, its rhythms, the idiosyncrasies of the land itself and its inhabitants. She has to work with the specific material that exists, shaping it, honouring it, bringing out its potential, according to her own vision and capabilities.

I will not go any further into matters of state here; the example of a Queen as head of a nation is useful in showing how the 'Queen of the Earth' archetype can be found in human society. We could just as easily say Empress, Duchess, Prime Minister, and the role can also be extended into the world of professional work – headmistress, chief executive, Matron, director. The Queen is, of course, also the individual woman. In everyday life, to step into the domain of the Queen of the Earth is to take full possession of one's bodily and sexual powers, and to meet the challenge of learning how best to manage them. A woman can learn about her own resources and cycles – the 'seasons' of her body and psyche – and use them to bring her projects to fruition. This may sound simple, but it is probably a lifetime's task. It can take many years to understand the rhythms of sexual desire, and of emotional tides. As a writer, for instance, I have to discover when I can write most fluently and coherently, but harness this into a reasonably regular schedule. If I try to write continuously, regardless of the time or the day, I exhaust myself and have only very patchy work to show for it. But if I wait for inspiration to strike, I will write only erratically, without continuity. What suits me may not suit you, and even when I have found a pattern that suits me, it may need to be varied from time to time. The cycle of feminine energy is tied in closely to the physical menstrual cycle, so that it is a priority for a woman in her reproductive years to know and attune herself to her cycle. There is a great deal of work that women can do in learning how to recognize, stimulate and channel various types of energies in their lives.

Understanding and handling personal resources is not, though, an end in itself, because sooner or later the question looms: 'What do you want to do with these powers when they are there for you to use?' In terms of the Queen of the Earth, the opportunity is then present to create a garden from the rawness of nature. We have come through the love of wild nature – the Princess stage – to the enthronement of the Queen, symbolizing the harnessing of the earth's resources. Now comes the stage when something more can be created, not only for practical use but as something of beauty in its own right. A garden is a personal statement. It carries the thought and design of the individual, yet it can flourish only if it is established in accord with natural forces. Plants have to be chosen that can tolerate the prevailing climate and type of soil. They must be regularly tended – a garden is not something that can be left alone; the stronger, rampant plants must be kept in check, weeds must be prevented from taking over, and the soil fed for healthy plants to grow.

A garden is not a purely female domain, but it has long been associated with the nature and beauties of woman. Again, in the Song of Solomon, we read:

A garden inclosed is my sister, my spouse; a spring shut up, a fountain sealed.
Thy plants are an orchard of pomegranates, with pleasant fruits . . .

(Chapter 4, verses 12, 13)

The Virgin Mary is often painted sitting in a rose garden, and in mystical Judaism the feminine presence in the world is likened to a garden, in which the King of Kings walks.

As we have moved through the different manifestations of the Queen of the Earth, we have come from a very generalized sense of nature, to a celebration of the basic fruiting cycles, to a specific, enhanced and cultivated area of land which we call a garden. When we grow, as individual women, we may feel a sense of loss that the years of innocence are gone, and that the years of heady sexuality are left behind. But we have a chance to be truly ourselves, to shape our individuality with artistry and intent.

Innocence, passion and wisdom can coexist as attributes of the Queen of the Earth. She must understand the barren phases, as well as the fertile ones, paying due tribute to the underworld, to the silence and darkness that reign there, as well as to the flourishing of new life through her desires. With the art and skill that come from her understanding, she can not only 'reproduce', but produce, shaping the magic garden after her own heart.

Images

Street Image

She appears to be bursting out of her clothes; it's not that they are too tight, more that her curves are too generous. Whatever the fashion, she favours low-cut bodices and a full-skirted dress. She has taken her shoes off, and is eating a ripe peach, wiping the juice from her chin with one hand, clutching a bag of fruit with the other. There is a summery look to her, whatever the time of year. She's easy with her companions – they're all laughing, and have a holiday air about them as they stroll through the park.

Mythic Image

A queen walking in her garden; she has an orchard which she visits, and gives the command for the fruit harvest to begin. Beyond the garden there are fields full of ripe corn, which she surveys with pleasure, and beyond that again a wild and hilly landscape where she sometimes rides with her companions. Artemis, Demeter, the Corn Goddess, the May Queen, the pregnant Virgin, the queens of our past history who have impressed themselves upon our land and culture.

Personal Image

There are times when you find a simple happiness, times when you are aware of your sexuality as a rich, dark tide. However many barren phases you go through, the fertility will return. What tasks do you carry out that put you in touch with the natural world or with raw materials? Do you ever want to take the process back a stage further – find wild fruit to cook? Dig the clay for pottery? Make vegetable dyes? What would the difference be if you did?

Evolution

Youth

First there is an unselfconscious relationship to nature. Later, there is a growing interest in the body, its powers of leaping, running, climbing, and then in its sexual development, growing breasts, pubic hair, and the filling out of bodily curves. The onset of menstruation, attended with much or little ceremony, according to culture, and later the first sexual experience, are the marking points.

Maturity

The woman may learn to give generously of herself, without giving her own self away. In maturity, she can enjoy her physicality, sensing the tides and currents of sexual energy there. Her menstrual cycles are a normal part of life, taken for granted, although their effects may change subtly over the years. She experiences renewals of sexual energy after periods of indifference, and learns to accept her rhythms, even though she cannot always predict them.

Old Age

She may become very wrinkled and withered – an aged tribeswoman squatting on her heels, half naked. Her daughters now carry on her line; her active sexual life is over, but she is still a power to be reckoned with and she can read the signs and omens of nature better than anyone else. She may be difficult to know and approach; she is not unhappy, but absorbed in her own being and the world of living nature around her.

Manifestations

Gifts

Physical fecundity, sexual appeal, ease of sexual arousal. An empathy with nature, 'green fingers' in the garden, a love of the changing seasons. An understanding of weather patterns, growth and harvest. The gift of fruitfulness, whatever the task.

Trials

Gluts – of fruit, lovers, sexual energy, offers of work, anything that pours in and leaves you struggling to cope with the flood. Equally, barrenness and infertility. Cold and harsh conditions, and times when nothing bears fruit.

Rituals and Cults

Ceremonies of the seasons, especially spring and harvest rituals. Feasts. Harvesting and storing produce, including bottling, jam-making etc. Rituals of menstruation, and of the sexual act.

The Vision

Of the inexhaustible cornucopia of life.

8

The Just Mother

In the heart of the Just Mother there is courage. She has the courage to look at what comes before her, recognize its nature, and stand firm upon the judgements that she makes. Such judgements may require that she take action, and this may involve warfare. To fulfil her role, she must both be objective and possess fighting skills. There is danger in her work, from without and within; she may attract antagonism or ridicule, and is also exposed to the force of her own strongest emotions, arising from her essential values of what is right and wrong.

Mythology contains many versions of the Just Mother, in both her fighting and her clear-seeing guises. In the Celtic tradition there were several war goddesses, often terrifying in appearance, possessed of supernatural powers by which they could influence the outcome of battles. The Roman goddess Minerva, allied to the Greek Athene, was associated both with war and with wisdom and clear thinking. Our own tradition still carries the emblem of Justice as a female figure bearing a sword and a pair of scales, presiding over courts of law. Today she is usually found blindfolded, probably signifying her impartiality, but until the sixteenth century she was always portrayed with her eyes open, emphasizing her far-reaching and penetrating gaze.

The making of judgements carries great responsibility. First the Just Mother sees, and then she judges, and from that judgement arises any action that she must take, or refrain from taking. When she makes her decision, she must stand by it, right or wrong, and accept the consequences. The cleaner the stroke of the sword, the more positive the outcome, no matter whether it is victory or defeat.

This can be illustrated by looking at the nature of accidents. In most cases, an accident is the outcome of a particular chain of cause and effect, and very often we have the chance to understand, at least in part, how it arose. This is not the same as apportioning blame, and suffering guilt. Indeed, blame, according to law or the eyes of the world, may lie in a very different direction. Suppose, for instance, you are driving in your car, and daydreaming. Another car pulls out of a side road in front of you and you crunch into the back of it. There is a clear moment in which you can accept the accident, with its cause and attendant effects. You know, in that instant, exactly why it happened, and you can choose to recognize the reason. In this particular case you know with certainty that if you had been properly alert, you would have been able to avoid the accident, although in law the other driver is at fault. Accepting this knowledge can be intensely painful. Immediately you are filled with the desire: 'If only I had looked ahead . . . if only I had been concentrating . . .' and so on. But the quicker you are able to accept that the deed is done, and cannot be undone, the more easily you will be able to deal with this knowledge, and the less complicated the after-effects are likely to be. This is the gift offered by the Just Mother, if we have the courage to accept it.

It may seem at first as though there was no decision-making involved in the accident, only a sequence of events that you can examine dispassionately. But perhaps you could find in that sequence the decision that caused you to daydream. Maybe you began to think about the holiday you were due to take next week, and you were wondering what the scenery would be like, whether you might make new friends, and so on. You chose to allow yourself to drift away from the present moment; it is not a crime, but in the moment of choice when you responded to the stirrings of your imagination, you set up conditions where there was a gap between conscious attention and physical co-ordination. This inevitably creates a time lapse between noticing what is happening on the road and reacting to it. In this case the time lapse was too great for you to be able to avoid an accident, even if it was only an extra second which might have made that critical difference. Nothing can be changed now, but it is still possible to see that a decision was made which led to the accident happening; if you can find the consciousness of that moment, then you have found the Just Mother.

It could be said that this example did not involve consequences which arose from an act of will, that, in other words, you did not 'intend' the accident to happen, that it came about more from an abdication of responsibility. But what if an accident arose from someone driving more aggressively than usual? Suppose the woman had a row with her husband before she got into the car. An accident happens: she then knows it was because she allowed her temper to get the better of her. Suppose she examines her actions conscientiously and finds out moreover that at a deeper level they arose from the decision: 'I am angry; someone must pay for it.' In one sense, she never intended to damage her own or anyone else's car; in another, having set that intention, those consequences followed. The consequences might have been different; they might not have involved a car accident; but when the intention is formed and the will set in motion, then there will be results of some sort or another. I remember reading a novel where a woman undergoing great stress had a car accident in which the driver of the other car was killed. When her husband and the police came to interview her in hospital, full of kindness and sympathy for her own injuries, ready to absolve her from blame if they possibly could, she answered their enquiries in only one way: 'I wanted to hit something'. They could not accept this, and put it down to the shock she was suffering, whereas, in fact, the shock had simply caused her to see right to the heart of the situation and know it for what it was.

All this may seem cold, clinical, and little to do with motherhood. At first, it might seem to be the antithesis of motherhood, which is to do with nourishing and rearing. In fact, the passing of judgement is at the same time one of the most essential and one of the most difficult aspects of motherhood. A mother has to judge the child which has been a part of her own physical being, and with whom she has an empathetic relationship. And when she has to take decisions to deny certain of the child's desires, or to punish bad behaviour, she is likely to feel his or her disappointment or misery in her own heart. To be effective in her role, she has to be sensitive to these feelings, but not completely identified with them; for the child's sake, she needs to stand firm in the position she has taken up.

This is an issue on which it is very hard to keep a balance when weighing up the conflicting claims of tolerance and discipline. Changing fashions in child care show that when one generation favours strictness, the next usually resorts to permissiveness. The over-strict approach can have the effect of dulling the mother's own sensitivity to her child; in this way, the relationship is distanced, so that she can exercise authority without too much discomfort. Such regimes are often accompanied by a vogue for impersonal birth procedures, restrictions on mother–child contact, severe feeding schedules, and a proscription on handling the baby unless essential. We tend to associate this with Western child care of the 1930s and 1940s, but echoes can be found in other modes of child rearing worldwide. Among the American Indians, for instance, babies were strapped to cradle-boards and hung in a distant tree if they cried; in Russia today they are plunged into icy-cold water to toughen them up.

The permissive routine (if it can be called such) may also benefit the mother more than the baby, for it relieves her of the responsibility of suffering for her child, since he is never to be denied. By gratifying all possible wishes, she spares herself the anguish of putting up with his displeasure and tears. It is hard to keep a balance between these two extremes; societies experiment with them both, and with all shades in between, and the prevailing customs can be influenced by a multitude of factors, such as environment, economy and national temperament.

Women may absorb received ideas of 'right' and 'wrong' ways to bring up children, but they will also have to make countless decisions in the moment. They have to judge whether to give or to withhold, whether to tolerate or reprimand. Children test the firmness of our decisions at every step of the way, and will use all the emotional ammunition they can to try to rock our certainty. It is a rare mother who never turns round and says, wearily, 'Oh, all right then! Go on!', but it is not sensible mothering to make a habit of that. Women who end up strained, nervous and over-tired are often those who cannot hold firm to a decision. Every issue becomes one which the child will try to circumvent, and the battles that are fought cause emotional upheaval on both sides, because the outcome lies in the balance every time. Becoming a mother means taking on authority, and being responsible for certain decisions.

There is no completely 'natural' way of bearing and rearing a child. Right from the start we make choices which further his or her life, or which can stunt or end it. There are choices to be made about diet and life-style during pregnancy, about infant feeding, schools, road safety, independence for the growing child, reading and television viewing. If, at the end of the process, there is a healthy, well-balanced adult, all we are able to say is that we made the choices which enabled that to be so.

Impersonality is present in passing judgement. In order to be fair, we have to cultivate impartiality, even with those we are closely bonded to and love most dearly. Perhaps this is another clue as to why Justice is female; she symbolizes the tenderness of affection that is not suppressed by judgement, but must be paired with the unselfishness of objectivity, creating the ability to stand back and decide what is best. Occasions can arise when a mother, loving her child intensely, may decide to give it up and let it be reared by another. Personal, family, even political circumstances can sometimes cause her to face such an agonizing decision, when she must try to judge what is best for the child, however much she loves it herself. And she in turn will be judged by others, for this is one of the inevitable consequences of making radical choices. However conscientiously she tried to make that decision, it is possible that the verdict will go against her in the eyes of the world.

Emotions

A sense of justice is closely linked to a sense of right and wrong. And this in turn is tied to strong personal emotions, which accompany our deepest convictions. A woman in the grip of a conviction is likely to carry more emotional power than a man; she may convince others through her utter sincerity, but she may also be attacked, for her emotional position exposes her, and leaves her less adaptable. Men, of course, have equally strong beliefs and values but they are less attached to the form that these take and more willing to modify them. Men can play with ideas; women become them.

This may be the reason for a general feminine reluctance to reveal personally held beliefs. Women may be more cautious about exposing themselves in this way, for their values are intricately bound up with what they do and who they are. A group of women who do not know each other very well, or individual women in men's company, tend to keep quiet about such things, at least until a level of trust has been built up. Those women who waste no time in stating their personal convictions often do so with exaggerated vehemence, as if they cannot be easy in spirit until everyone else has agreed with them.

I think this can be a lack of courage on our, the women's, part. We complain that men's views hold sway, when we do not look for a realistic way of advancing our own. We want to put forward our beliefs only when we are reasonably sure that everyone else will assent to them, or at least pretend to. And we also sometimes lack the courage to look closely at those beliefs, to subject them to public debate, and to be willing for them to be modified.

Our emotional drives, and sense of identity, can be embedded in a belief structure, and we can fear that cool reason may overturn the whole thing. This stems partly from a justified wariness that other people may apply only harsh logic and forget completely the emotional element and the presence of compassion, imagination and intuition as ingredients of human life. However, if there is real knowledge at the core of our beliefs, then the shortcomings of such an analysis cannot shake that knowledge; we should not need to have our confidence sustained by external support.

The emotional stratum that encloses the network of beliefs is an important one, particularly if it can be liberated from the tyranny of self-protection that I have just described. It is the source of a passionate caring about life. It is a fuel which can be ignited to give impetus to our missions and quests. All the so-called 'negative' emotions can actually be turned to good account in this way. Anger, fear and grief are all sources of energy that can be converted to positive use. A sense of perspective is needed so that these emotions are used economically and to best possible effect. I remember one occasion when I wanted to complain about some faulty repair work on a domestic item. I was filled with fury and a kind of self-pity that I had paid good money and been shabbily treated. (Indeed I felt it was I who had been so treated, rather than the object.) I then agonized over whether to complain or not, imagining my humiliation if my claim were rejected. In the middle of this ridiculous scenario I suddenly realized that all I had to do was to decide in my own mind that the work had not been done properly, that it was quite correct for me to complain, and then to go in to the shop calmly, but with determination and conviction. It was perfectly simple; I met with a positive response and there was no rudeness or ill-feeling on either side.

Facing the World

Every time a woman knows what she wants, and is prepared to go out and stake her claim for it, she pushes back the frontiers of her world a little further. Sometimes these are just her personal boundaries, but sometimes she contributes towards changing the prevailing view of what a woman can and should do. Perhaps this is the equivalent of men's pioneering activities – discovering new continents, exploring space, climbing new heights, and so on. Women pioneer through extending their self-image and the scope of their activities.

This liberation is far from being a modern phenomenon. Oddly enough, it seems that the challenge of liberation is one that faces us in every age. There is always a weight of tradition that we wish to lighten, there are always conventions and expectations that we want to stretch. In some centuries, for instance, women manage to shake off the view that they should not be learned, or write. In an ecclesiastical world dominated by men, certain medieval nuns emerged as scholars and mystics, including poets and authors of high repute such as Abbess Hildegard of Bingen (see pages 134–135), Julian of Norwich, and St Theresa of Avila. In England, the Tudor period provided an easy climate for women to attain education, but by the Elizabethan era, and in the century following, women once again had to struggle for a literary voice; the seventeenth-century poetess, Anne Kingsmill, wrote wryly:

> Did I my lines intend for publick view
> How many censures, wou'd their faults pursue . . .
> Alas! a woman that attempts the pen
> Such an intruder on the rights of men
> Such a presumptuous Creature, is esteem'd
> The fault, can by no virtue be redeem'd.

Nowadays, once again, education for women is largely accepted in the West. In many ways, our society is exceptionally liberated, as far as women's position goes. However, there are certain areas in which we do not at present involve ourselves, even though these have been colonized by women in the past. We have almost no trace of the 'warrior' tradition, for instance, whereas, in medieval times, it was common for women to be in charge of defending the homestead and of fighting in any sieges if their husbands were away from home. Some women even fought in the Crusades, and literature and folk history are full of tales of women dressing as male soldiers and sailors and showing as much courage in war as the men. On the whole, this is not a privilege that we crave today.

It may be held that war is man's invention, and that women left to themselves are purely peace-loving and co-operative creatures. I am not so sure about this. Perhaps organized warfare, with military manoeuvres, uniforms, and weapons of wide-scale destruction, are a masculine invention. But women will certainly fight when there is a need. In the animal kingdom, the mother will fight to the death to protect her offspring (the female is often the more deadly of the species), whereas warring male animals tend to stop short of killing one another; it is a display of power and aggression that will go through several set stages of warning before physical fighting even begins, and is not normally a fight to the death.

Most human mothers would physically fight to defend their babies and children. In addition, social groups, such as the medieval households mentioned, and certain 'primitive' tribes, organize themselves so that when the men are away at war or hunting, the women can protect the castle or village. They are trained to use weapons, and to co-ordinate their defence. There is a role for the woman as warrior; just because we do not often need to invoke it in a physical sense in today's society does not mean that its potential has died away. Perhaps it is the case that women fight to defend, whereas men fight to attack.

Our battles, nowadays, are usually on levels other than the physical and, as I have already suggested, can be to do with establishing territory in a changing world. Women's psyche is strongly linked to a sense of space and place, and it seems that we have to forever define and re-define that space.

This is not intended to give a pessimistic view of women's position, but to imply that each new phase of society makes demands upon us, which we must meet by stepping beyond the bounds of previously imposed restrictions. To do so needs courage, and an inner sense of worth, since mockery and hatred can accompany the efforts of women to extend their world. To carry this through undaunted, a woman needs to be confident of her values, and of what she thinks is worth struggling for, because she will not necessarily meet with a favourable response from the world at large.

A woman who makes a public stand often seems to be the object of more mockery, in fact, than a man. Any crack in her dignity is seized upon and used to ridicule her, and any quirk of personality exaggerated into a caricature; this is immediately obvious if you think of any female campaigner or politician. A woman's image is stronger than a man's (compare the individuality of female fashion, for instance, with the anonymity of male attire) and is therefore easier to exaggerate and deride. This gives women in public life an added source of power, for they can make an impression through their image, but it can also be a source of pain unless they can view the situation coolly and recognize that their image is an outward show and not their complete person.

When we push back the frontiers, we will inevitably encroach upon 'no-go' areas for females. Strongly held beliefs of what women should and should not do are touched on, and resistance often comes from among other women themselves. Thus a new style of activity for women can bring protests that such behaviour is unfeminine, and that women are turning themselves into men. Necessity of circumstances is often a dissolver of such views; in the First and Second World Wars, for instance, it became essential to the national economy that women should drive buses, take over businesses and wear trousers. A cry of 'unfeminine' may in fact be replaced by a new awareness of femininity. Female abilities are given scope, and sexuality is enhanced. There is a sexiness about women wearing men's clothes, for instance, as they can emphasize the feminine rather than obliterate it. An American feature film, *Willa*, followed the attempts of a young woman to break into the male world of truck-driving, and was cleverly shot so that the more strong and earthy she appeared, the more her vulnerability and attractiveness came through. This is not to suggest that women engage in 'masculine' activities in order to titillate the male sex, but certainly it sometimes causes them to be seen in a new light, and this, when the shock waves have died down, actually heightens femininity and acts like a breath of fresh air to the stuffy, conventional female image that always becomes too set in time.

Weapons

The weapons used by a woman in a struggle are, on the whole, different from those used by men. At the very least, they may be applied differently. The word 'heroine' has quite a different flavour from 'hero'. A quality of bravery is common to both, but that is where the similarity ends. Female physical strength is not normally equivalent to male strength, and so other ways of fighting have to be found; this is not a second-best response, for women can call on inner strengths of their own to help them through a fight.

The term 'weapon' should be taken broadly, not just to mean an instrument of physical destruction. There is a parallel in the magical tradition where 'weapon' is a term used not only for agents of force, such as knife and axe, but for any instrument that represents a power that can be used to further a chosen end. A cup, for instance, can be a magical weapon; it can represent love, and love is a supreme strength that can win through against the most towering difficulties.

I shall suggest just three qualities which seem to be predominantly female strengths in a fighting context. I shall assume, too, that we are talking about a struggle for a worthwhile cause, rather than methods of injuring others. These qualities are persistence, cleverness and precision. They are not exclusive to the female sex, but they are skills which women can and must learn to exercise in battle if they are to deal with opponents of greater force.

In the male–female arena, home of so many struggles, persistence is a weapon which many a woman has used. The girl Willa, heroine of the feature film mentioned above, finally got her own way in being allowed to drive lorries simply by asking again and again and refusing to take 'No' for an answer. Men usually expect women to take 'No' for an answer, particularly if they say it forcefully enough. But a woman can decide not to be washed up by that particular tidal wave; she can present her case again, and again, if needs be, choosing her moments carefully. If she allows herself to be untouched by opposition, and repeats her move forward, she has a good chance of breaking through when the opposing forces have spent their strength. This applies not only to one-to-one situations, male and female, but also to circumstances where a woman has to confront 'authority' in the form of committees, boards, bureaucrats, and so on.

A sense of timing is important. Taking the wave analogy further, it is like using the ebb and flow of the water to proceed, instead of being knocked sideways by the force of a breaking wave. Persistence also implies patience, and patience itself can be a kind of courage, the willingness to wait, to hold on and not be discouraged by the difficulties. It is an act of keeping faith. Sometimes this can apply to a relationship, where a woman may choose to keep her commitment, despite almost insuperable odds, and yet win through in the end. Stories of women waiting years for their lovers to return, such as the Greek tale of Penelope awaiting Ulysses, or that of the unnamed heroine of English folk-song, who passes seven faithful years until her lover comes back from sea, may not have immediate psychological appeal. They seem to stretch credibility to its limits. But perhaps they are not describing real-life situations, at least in the literal sense; they are, rather, emblems for the faith and endurance which enable love finally to flourish after a period of utmost aridity.

The ability to hold on and to wait is emphasized as essential to women's development, in a Nootka Indian myth of initiation. A young girl, last possessor of the Old Magic of the women, is washed up on inhospitable land and must survive there:

The old magic, what she knew of it, was safe ... this had happened before, and each time, when it was Time, that which was needed had been found, that which had been forgotten had been re-learned. Or given. To Endure was all that was required of her.

And she endured. Endured ... She Endured. And survived. Marginally, perhaps, but it is not required of us that we live well. Throughout the long wet winter, even when the snow lay deep on the mountain and ice blocked the rivulets, she Endured. Throughout the following spring and summer, drying berries and finding the nests of birds, scavenging and surviving, she Endured.

(Anne Cameron, *Daughters of Copper Woman*)

Precision is related to persistence, in that it involves wise use of timing and energy, in order not to be defeated by strength that is superior in terms of output. This is a good fighting tactic in any case; a well-aimed blow from a Karate expert can wreak more havoc than a full-blooded fist fight. But precision is a skill that it is imperative for women to develop, in order to combat greater force. When we use words as weapons, there is often a natural tendency to pour out a torrent of exhortation, recrimination, or abuse. Not only can men shout louder, but, in fact, shouting is far less effective than delivering a few carefully chosen words, which make more impact, and carry more conviction.

Precision requires that we know exactly what we aim to achieve. The setting of intention relates to the gathering of will and is thus vitally important. If the aim, the intention, can be formulated clearly and adhered to, then one is more likely to be able to cut a clean passage through the opposing forces. This leaves freedom for the actual details of the operation to be worked out at each successive stage, since a firm intention is not the same as making exact plans, and, in fact, it may have a better chance of fulfilment if one is able to adapt to changing circumstances as they arise.

To find the right way of doing this, we need our wits about us. Cleverness is a vital feminine weapon; where men prefer to charge in with muscle power and bravado, women must be canny and sharp-witted. Theseus would still be blundering about in the maze if Ariadne had not supplied him with a thread so that he could find his way out. The myth concerning these two is a beautiful example of the difference between hero and heroine, and how they can use their individual abilities to complement each other.

Once again, received folk wisdom on this matter speaks loud and clear. In the British ballad tradition there are several songs about how women outwitted dangerous men, or tested their loyalty. In the first category is 'The Outlandish Knight', the story of a murderer, a handsome young man who persuades a girl to run away with him in the dead of night, taking her family's money with her as a dowry. Arriving at a river which they must cross, he forces her off her horse and gives her the blood-curdling news that he has drowned seven pretty maidens here and she is to be the eighth. He demands that she strip off her clothes and hand over to him all her goods. She cunningly replies that he must turn his back, since if she must die, she will do so with her modesty intact! This gives her the chance to push him into the river and make her escape, and she is safely back in bed before the members of her household are any the wiser. Only the household parrot, the magic talking bird, has to be bribed into silence with promises of a fine new cage made of silver and gold.

Another ballad, 'The Female Highwayman', concerns an enterprising young lady called Sylvie, who decides to test her lover's commitment to her. She dresses up as a highwayman, 'with sword and pistol by her side', and lies in wait for him. When she threatens him and demands that he hand over his money, he quakingly agrees. However, when she asks for the ring that he is wearing, he musters his courage, saying that he would rather die than part with it, since it was given to him by his true love. Satisfied, Sylvie removes her disguise and the story comes to a happy end.

It may be thought that, in matters of weapons and fighting, men are the natural superiors, and that women must make shift as best they can. Traditionally, this is not the case. It is true that men fight most of the physical battles on the earth, but women have long been associated with the power of weapons, and with initiating men into the skills of battle. In early Scandinavian and German custom, a son always received his sword from his mother, and there are legends, such as those in Arthurian mythology, indicating that possession of supreme weapons can only come about through female assistance. King Arthur's sword, Excalibur, is connected with the Lady of the Lake, who in turn is associated with Morgan le Fay, a woman with an ambiguous role in legend being both a black enchantress and a healer and lady of wisdom. Magic and fighting are closely connected; the Welsh hero Peredur receives his initiation in an enchantresses' palace, where he learns the complete range of knightly arts, and the skills of handling weapons, in just three weeks!

This short description of some of the feminine strengths in fighting gives food for thought as to the 'weapons' and skills which form a part of female knowledge. They can actually be passed on and taught to men, to refine and sharpen their strengths, and such generosity, expressed in myth, is reassuring. It shows how the sexes may give to one another, rather than use their knowledge to stand against each other.

Beyond the Battle

The Just Mother can choose not to enter into battle at all. This is not the same as avoiding conflict; the choice can signify a state where all the possibilities of battle are seen and accepted, but in order for a higher level of interaction to take place, they are transcended. The best way to explain this is to describe how it can happen in practice. Communication is a good example; the usual procedure in debate, both in masculine and in mixed contexts, is the use of the 'cut and thrust' method. Arguments may be heated and forceful, and the aim can be to override one's opponent (as he is often seen to be).

This does not suit women well. Women can certainly argue fiercely, but this touches emotional nerves, and provokes strong defensive reactions to protect personal values. To men, a verbal battle is enjoyable and a good war game; to women it is not. In mixed company this kind of procedure can be very threatening, and often the only way to make a point seems to be by being more vehement and shrill than the men. The easy way out is simply to avoid all confrontation. This prevents immediate trouble – but it does not allow for any real exchange of ideas.

It is possible, however, to go right beyond the battling stage (as it is normally conducted) to a level where knowledge is evaluated and shared calmly and objectively. For this to be the case, individuals must be self-disciplined. The person proposing an idea must be concise and committed to putting it forward. The listeners must give their full attention, and avoid tangential trains of thought; they must allow the ideas to resound in the space of their own minds, and indeed their hearts, accepting any responses that arise, but not being dominated by them. Reactions of anger, enthusiasm and so on are natural when one is listening to stimulating ideas, but riding these emotions means stopping short of truly appraising them.

If this can be achieved in a group of women, and also if it can be brought in some measure into a mixed situation, then a very special quality can be present. It is lucid, spacious and intelligent. I have seen it operating in certain contexts where there is a high degree of personal responsibility and mutual respect, and it is a quality not easily forgotten. Rather than complaining that men do not let us have our say, we must learn to develop these skills and introduce them into the everyday world. The present shouting matches known as British Parliamentary sessions are far from ideal; now that women are becoming more prominent in the world of politics, we have an opportunity to change this state of affairs.

Images

Street Image

A tall, keen-eyed woman, moving confidently through the crowd. She carries a smart briefcase, which might carry a court brief or political documents. She puts in some spare time working for Legal Aid or Citizens Rights, but at the moment, in her lunch hour, she is on her way to the electrical shop to return a faulty personal dictaphone. Her knowledge of rights, guarantees and procedures is impeccable; she can never be faulted on these.

Mythic Image

The goddesses of war and justice – the Celtic Morrigan, the avenging Furies, Minerva. Emblems of Justice; the seated woman with sword and scales; Portia in Shakespeare's *Merchant of Venice*. Warrior women – Joan of Arc, Boudicca, the Amazons. A mighty figure, fierce in battle, calm and dignified in repose, ready to dispense justice dispassionately.

Personal Image

You know that you are right – or do you? Think again. If you are convinced, then you need have no fear of opposition, because you can win through like a blade cutting through melting ice. In moments of calm, contemplate the chain of cause and effect. How far can you follow it back, and what is the point that prevents you from seeing further? What spheres of your life do you have authority in? Are you comfortable about using it?

Evolution

Youth

Raised on stories of bravery, our young heroine wants to challenge the school bully, own up when she is wrong, and rescue the geography teacher from mortal danger. When this gets too much for everyone else, then they may give her the part of Joan of Arc in the school play to mop up her zeal. In reality, the young girl will find herself in situations now and again where she is powerless to act against unfairness; she can only weep in secret, but remembers these incidents with a smouldering anger well into adult life. Groups of girls and adolescents hold frequent courts of justice where they scrutinize each other's behaviour and that of their boyfriends and parents. The verdict is often 'Guilty'.

Maturity

The woman falls under the discipline of her job, of bringing up her children. She has no choice but to make decisions, and is sometimes called upon to defend them. She may sometimes surprise herself by the decisions she makes, which run counter to previous expectations and conditioning. The roles of manager, instructor and team leader may come her way both in the professional world and in the home, as she discovers new authority in herself which she can use with confidence.

Old Age

An indomitable old lady. She is fair, but you cannot swerve her from her decision unless you can prove beyond a shadow of doubt that you are right. Her mind is crystal clear, her politics well thought-out but by now a little rigid. She keeps an interest in what is happening in the world at large. Irascible, impatient, totally unsentimental, but children love her because she treats them as individual people worthy of respect.

Manifestations

Gifts

Certainty. Strength of purpose. Detachment and objectivity. An eye for the truth of a situation. Friends in high places who will lend their influence when necessary. Others of like mind who will work with you on a cause. A good education and the power to articulate your purpose, which will lend skill to your efforts. The loyalty of others.

Trials

Scorn and rejection. Accusations of not being feminine, of putting politics or the welfare of others before one's own family. Endurance of harsh conditions. Trickery and treachery. Experiencing injustice which one is powerless to remedy.

Rituals and Cults

Women's self-defence programmes. The training of women in the police force and in the armed forces. Protest groups and women's peace groups. Rescue activities – for example, the Samaritans. Historical women's movements, such as the Suffragettes. Work on the frontiers of the feminine – the first woman to go to university, wear trousers, go into space, join all-male organizations. Informal courts of justice where women assemble socially to discuss rights and wrongs of politics, child care, and the actions of others.

The Vision

Of the law of consequence, and our role in shaping it.

9

The Lady of the Dance

Imagine a dream where you are dancing, with springy, rhythmical steps, responding eagerly to half-heard music. There are vibrant, cheerful notes from a violin, and perhaps sweeter, more poignant chords from a harp. The music picks up tempo, and the energetic rhythms begin to toss you in the air till you are bounding higher and higher. You are dancing gracefully, it seems, in the air itself, laughing, spinning in arcs and spirals of movements, just as you have always longed to do. Now you are flying, dancing as the specks of dust in a shaft of light or the stars in the sky. But while you are joyfully and totally absorbed in the dance, the music comes back loudly to your ears. It is now harsh and discordant, and your body becomes heavy and awkward. You sink to the ground again and feel so weighed down that you cannot move at all; you try to stretch out an arm, but have no power to do so. Immobile as stone, you are rooted to the earth.

This flight of dream fancy is echoed in certain folk tales, particularly those connected with stone circles in Britain and on the Continent. The stones of some of these circles, such as the Merry Maidens in Cornwall, are described as young women whose ecstatic dancing was halted because it took place on the Sabbath. The 'maidens' were frozen into stone, and remain there still, unable to continue their dance. Scholars say that these myths may reflect a conflict between the demands of early Christianity and ancient practices of using stone circles for dancing rituals. Whatever their origin, the stories can give us the uncanny sense that within each stone is a dancer, waiting to be released from long suspense; a dance, held in a moment of stillness, that will one day burst forth again into movement, to celebrate the spinning of heaven and earth.

The Lady of the Dance is the spirit of this dance. She is the one who delights to know the world through movement, to infect others with the joy of dancing, to capture the changing colours of light, in mood and gesture. She is provocative, graceful, exuberant and free; she poses a threat to those who only understand a fixed order, and she may be cast into captivity by them.

Dancing in our Lives

In her book, *A Soprano on Her Head*, Eloise Ristad talks about recapturing a spontaneous and joyful approach to the performing arts. She believes that such an approach is inborn in most of us, and that, as children, we instinctively move to music, but that very often 'education' and our own self-consciousness freeze the dance, so that we lose this pleasure. She does not deny the need for technique and discipline, but points out the danger that these might kill the very spirit they are meant to enhance. I feel that I might encounter the same problem in another form if I were to try to make painstaking analogies between 'dance' and 'real life' all the way through this chapter. So I should prefer to write about the aspects of dance that seem most relevant to the archetype of the Lady of the Dance, and leave readers to draw their own parallels.

However, first there are some general observations to make about the role of dance in our lives. It might be said that the progress of each individual life is like the unfolding of a musical symphony, which only that person can hear. We alone create the steps which we dance to our music; we must learn to be our own choreographers. There is a proverb: 'They who dance are thought mad by those who hear not the music'. In dance, there is continual change of movement, gracefully expressed, and this gives us an indication of how we can handle changes in our own lives. To meet the variations in the music, which are like changes in circumstances or in our own state of being, we need

poise, alertness and co-ordination. Above all, to create a dance of
beauty and vitality, we need to take pleasure in it. We need to
have a willingness to respond joyfully to the music, however
'mad' this may sometimes seem to others. Acting on impulse,
responding to surprise, allowing enthusiasm to take hold of us,
are new bursts of energy in the dance.

For women, this implies that we should not let the urge to
order dominate our lives. Organizing, tidying, making and keeping routines have an essential place in life for most of us; we are
'multi-active' creatures, keeping up with different responsibilities
and, of necessity, streamlining tasks. We dread mess and chaos,
which makes us feel unable to cope. But if a fixity of order takes
precedence, we can cut off our natural birthright – a pleasure in
the dance of life.

This pleasure is not by any means the privilege of the better-
off woman, or the one who has most time on her hands.
Traditionally, a women's manual and domestic work has been
accompanied by singing and dancing. Indonesian women, tired
after a stint working in the fields, refresh themselves by taking a
break for dancing. Closer to home, until recent times, Hebridean
women making tweed ('waulking' the cloth), accompanied themselves with rhythmic singing, to ease and enliven the burden of
the work. If we no longer have the opportunity for weaving song
and dance into the pattern of our working lives, then we must
seek other activities which will have the same effect of revitalizing
flagging spirits and giving pent-up energy an outlet.

A friend of mine was recently feeling exhausted, drained and
generally weary of life after the birth of her last baby. She faced
the problems of coping with several children and a full-time job,
but was urged by her husband to do more, rather than less. She
(quite naturally) found his advice somewhat callous, but eventually agreed to try re-joining some of her evening classes. To
her amazement, she broke through the barrier of fatigue and
regained much of her old happiness and energy. It is when we
are governed only by the 'Must do this' and 'Ought to see to that'
factors of life that we lose the pleasure in it; sometimes an 'I'm
going to do this' or 'I want to do that' can transform matters.

Ladies of the Dance

In classical mythology, the Graces, attendants of Venus (Aphrodite), were closely associated with the dance. Their role was to bring 'sweetness and charm' to life, and they were three in number. Their usual names were Aglaia, the Bright One, Euphrosyne, the Glad One, and Thaleia, the One of Abundance. Their dance evoked the awakening of spring on the earth, and they were thought to inspire the forming of buds on the trees, the opening of blossom, and the ripening of fruits. They were also said to be the goddesses of gratitude. This is a striking attribution, for the joy of dancing comes from a gratitude for the gift of life itself. An ode by Pindar, dating from the fifth century BC, contains the following praise of the Graces:

> You whose portion
> Is beside the waters of Kephisos,
> Who live where fine horses abound,
> O song-celebrated,
> Queenly Graces of Orchomenos the fertile,
> O watchers over the ancient Minyans,
> Listen. Listen to my prayers. For it is you
> Who help men to all
> That is sweet and delightful,
> Whether it is the skill of a man, or
> His looks or his fame.
> For not even the gods
> Can command their dances and banquets if the holy
> Graces are absent, who are the housewives
> Of all things in heaven, enthroned alongside
> The god with the bow
> Of gold, Pythian Apollo, revering the eternal
> Lordship of the Olympian Father . . .
>   (Quoted in Geoffrey Grigson, *The Goddess of Love*)

It is likely that it is these three Graces that we see in Botticelli's famous painting, *La Primavera* ('The Spring'). Three beautiful young women, dressed in gauzy robes, are pictured dancing gracefully in a circle, their hands clasped together. Each handhold occurs at a different level – one above the head, one at shoulder height, and one at hip level. Botticelli, familiar with Renaissance neo-Platonic teaching, may well have intended this grouping to represent the harmony of the three different forces of Creation. These three forces may be described in various ways, and form a central part of the teaching of other philosophies, such as the Cabbala; in the present context we could call them the initiating, the resisting, and the unifying or balancing. The three forces are said to be at the heart of all created forms, animate or inanimate, visible or invisible, and to give the continual impulse to the movement of life itself.

In dancing, they can be seen taking place as follows. The dancer makes a movement with her foot, lifting it up into the air; this corresponds to the initiating force. She continues the arc of movement till her foot descends again, meeting the resistance of the ground below – the second force. Her body then adjusts its movement to 'balance' this resistance, producing, if she is a good dancer, a beautiful effect. Thus the three forces in dance can be perceived as the impulse to movement, the encounter with limitations (which may be ground surface, furthest extent of bodily movement, gravity, and so on), and the harmonizing of the response into a new posture or further movement.

The three may work together almost simultaneously, and their constant interaction will produce the flow of the dance. We could take this one stage further and say that the initiating force represents the energy of the dance, the resisting force leads to rhythm, and the unifying force creates the actual form of the dance. Let us consider these in turn.

Energy in Dance

The quality of the energy that feeds the dance of the Lady of the Dance is sparkling and playful. It is the kind that encourages you to skip, rather than to walk sedately. Dance is accompanied by a joyful release of energy, whether the movement into which it is channelled is sad or cheerful in mood, fast or slow. Such energy can often be involved irrespective of one's current physical state; as I mentioned, women tired from hard labouring can take to dance to renew their strength. Most of us will have had the experience of going to a party or dance convinced that we were far too exhausted even to lift a foot to the music, but instead found ourselves leaping about like spring lambs. It seems that, in an extraordinary way, dancing can link physical movement with the essential vitality of our beings, drawing on a kind of underground stream of energy and sending it up as a bubbling fountain.

This energy may not be in the least refined; it can be raw and raunchy. It may also be almost childlike, a current feeding the imagination and transforming the world around. There is a similarity to the play of children, too, in that dance requires total involvement in the moment. In literal terms, a movement is made and then is gone for ever. In her mind, too, the dancer must forget the step she has just danced and stay with the present one; if she congratulates or blames herself for what she has just done, she is likely to lose impetus for the movements she is making now. If she thinks too far ahead, it is likely to detract from her performance. With casual dancing, this sense of the moment is very apparent as you are simply responding to whatever the music brings, without any thought of a sequence of movements. In more stylized dance, the movements may well be completely choreographed, but then the dancer will have learnt them so thoroughly that she can still respond to the demands of each moment, trusting her memory and training to guide her through the rest.

The energy of dance can transform people in a remarkable way. Very often, someone who looks heavy and slow turns out to be a light and fluent dancer, and the over-serious shed their gravity and thoroughly enjoy themselves. Dancing seems to create more physical energy, but even when this, too, is used up, the dancers may find that they are left with more mental and emotional energy, a cheerful and relaxed outlook which they can take into other areas of life.

Rhythm

Rhythm is the basic ordering factor of dance; it creates a structure of repetition where the pulse of the dance is understood. If I know, for example, that the beat of the dance is one strong beat followed by two lighter ones at regular intervals, then my body can respond to that of its own accord. The body itself is a creature of rhythm; it has a heart-beat, and many other subtle pulses as well. There are rhythms of renewal and decay; there are rhythms in the brain, in sleep, and in emotional life too.

As I have suggested, rhythm represents the second, or resisting, force, and it can create many different effects. A dance rhythm can be intensely exciting, or sexually arousing, or almost hypnotic. It can be heavy or light, simple or intricate. It could be said that rhythm marks the change-points, where energy is either arrested or given another boost, and that the pattern of holding back and impulsion creates specific rhythmic effects. We are able to change our mood by dancing to a particular rhythm, and it may well be that different rhythms stimulate certain centres in us. For instance, a very complex rhythm may stimulate the mental faculties, because it is not easily grasped, and we cannot help but try to 'make sense' of its pattern. Other types may trigger off emotional or instinctive responses. Ever since the time of the Greeks, concern has been expressed about the effects rhythm may have. An extreme view in the modern age comes from the pen of Cyril Scott:

After the dissemination of Jazz, which was definitely 'put through' by the Dark Forces, a very marked decline in sexual morals became noticeable. Whereas at one time women were content with decorous flirtations, a vast number of them are now constantly preoccupied with the search for erotic adventures, and have thus turned sexual passion into a species of hobby. Now, it is just this over-emphasis of the sex-nature, this wrong attitude towards it, for which Jazz-music has been responsible. The orgiastic element about its syncopated rhythm, entirely divorced from any more exalted musical content, produced a hyper-excitement of the nerves, and loosened the powers of self-control. It gave rise to a false exhilaration, a fictitious endurance, an insatiability resulting in a deleterious *moral* and physical reaction.

(C. Scott, *Music – its Secret Influence Through the Ages*, Rider, 1933)

Although we may find this response excessively condemnatory, nevertheless it makes some interesting points. The basic message, that rhythms create effects and we must take responsibility for the rhythms we create, has some value, even if we would not see general promiscuity as the inevitable result of syncopated ('off-beat') rhythms. The issue is not dead; even more recently it was raised by a writer who was courageous enough to question whether exposure to frequent bursts of 'rock' music could have the effect of dulling our senses and destroying the possibility of entering into more exalted forms of emotional and spiritual consciousness. It is interesting that this immediately produced an outcry; the impression I gained was that very few people were prepared to assert that rhythm and music can really affect us for better or worse and that the question of discriminating between them raised a great deal of fear. And yet many societies have carefully structured different rhythmic forms of music and dance, ordaining that each has their own suitability for different times and places – the temple, the court, the folk dance, and so on – and that each will tend to create certain effects upon the listener. The message from history seems to be that we can distinguish between these effects and harness them to desirable ends, dismissing those which are harmful. The reluctance to make such judgements that we encounter today is more closely bound up, I suspect, with the fear that ulterior motivations may creep in if such discrimination is exercised, and that governments may try to assert political control, for instance, through music promotion and censorship.

However, to refuse to look at the issue at all is avoiding taking any responsibility for the music and dance forms we create and encourage; it also closes the door on a whole area of potential. It would be better, surely, to open up the debate, and research these questions in depth.

After all, we know already that certain rhythms can actually cause harm. One of the methods of Chinese torture was said to be to use the sound of water, dripping often enough to be noticeable, but not so frequently as to make sense as a regular rhythm; the struggles of the brain to anticipate the next drop were said to produce a state of torment. We all know that a loud and unwelcome rhythm, even a ticking clock, can be a source of great irritation, disturbing thought or sleep. This seems to be because we respond to rhythm, like it or not; we anticipate the coming beat and feel the pulse within ourselves.

In the rhythm of daily life we may also have a chance to create new rhythms which will produce different effects in our general mode of existence. A pattern of life with a dull, steady, insistent rhythm could perhaps be improved by a more sprightly beat. A life with an insecure, fragmented rhythm could be less draining of energy if a more orderly pulse were created. Conversations, work and sexual relationships all have an intrinsic rhythm which can be varied or intensified as we choose.

The Dance Form

Dance is an exploration of possibilities. It involves, potentially, every possible extension of muscle and limbs, every conceivable point of balance, and all achievable combinations of movement. Each particular form of dance has its own characteristics and specialities, so that ballet, for instance, uses frequent graceful extensions of arms, neck and legs, whereas belly-dancing involves vigorous movements of the hips, and folk dances energetic rhythms for the feet. Dance invites us to explore unusual but harmonious ways of reconciling opposites, just as the third 'balancing' force marries impulse and resistance. The forms we create will have particular qualities which can convey emotional and spiritual truth. In a spontaneous dance, these qualities are present and then dissolve, but in a structured form they can be recreated in the same manner on other occasions. If such a form has an underlying framework which can be understood by other people, then the dance can be shared and communicated.

Traditionally, specific cultural and religious qualities have been associated with certain dance forms. In the Renaissance, the pavane, danced in a slow triple measure, was a dance form of great dignity, often used for processions and high ceremony. The galliard, on the other hand, was a nimble and inventive dance, with a catchy, tricky rhythm. The courtier dancing it was expected to show individual wit and agility, with spectacular leaps to make the onlookers gasp. In the masque form, an entertainment popular right through the seventeenth century, an elaborate arrangement of allegorical song and action was accompanied by dances, the whole spectacle often describing a kind of cosmos in miniature, inhabited by gods, mortals, fairies, beasts and the like. Its centre was symbolized by the visiting sovereign or nobility, who were present as audience, and who were expected to enliven the performance at the end by joining in the dances themselves. An amusing account is left to us by Orazio Busino, a visiting Italian, who was present at the masque, 'Pleasure Reconciled to Virtue', in 1618:

Last of all they danced the spagnoletta, one at a time, each with his lady, and being well nigh tired they began to lag, whereupon the King, who is naturally choleric, got impatient and shouted aloud, 'Why don't we dance? What did you make me come here for? The devil take you all – dance!' Whereupon, the Marquis of Buckingham, His Majesty's favourite, immediately sprang forward, cutting a score of lofty and very minute capers with so much grace and agility that he not only appeased the ire of his angry lord but rendered himself the admiration and delight of everybody. The other masquers, thus encouraged, continued to exhibit their prowess, one after another, with various ladies, also finishing with capers and lifting their goddesses from the ground.
(Quoted in *Four Hundred Songs and Dances from the Stuart Masque*, edited by Andrew J. Sabol, Brown University Press, USA, 1978)

Each form of dance serves a specific purpose, even though dance itself arises from a natural urge simply to dance for the love of it. A dance is constructed to serve its purpose best, even though we may never question why we do a waltz or a country dance or tap dancing. Some dances, such as those to rock music, may be primarily for releasing energy. Very many are to do with men and women getting to know each other. It occurred to me when I was at a barn dance, that this was a splendid way for members of the opposite sex in a village community to size each other up. We were engaged in a dance sequence where each lady moved to a different man in turn and was spun around by him, and it was remarkable how varied the physical sensations were in the hands of the different men. Some partners would give you a vigorous spin – too vigorous in certain cases – while others were limp and ineffective! In a community where men and women could interact socially, but where any physical contact was closely circumscribed, these dances would give one a very direct sense of a man's physical being without the slightest impropriety. At more refined levels of society, this also went on; eighteenth- and nineteenth-century novels are full of ballroom scenes in which critical developments of plot hang on invitations and refusals to dance, the behaviour of the key characters on the dance floor, and brief but intimate conversations made possible by the rare opportunity for a couple to be at physical close quarters.

The Message of the Dance

Returning to Botticelli's painting, *La Primavera*, it is possible that the three other women in the picture represent the different stages of the development of the goddess Venus. The one naked, except for a transparent veil grasped by a winged and amorous pursuer, would be Venus in her lowest personification, that of desire. The middle one, La Primavera herself, represents abundance and love; and the one furthest away signifies the ultimate union of love. The Lady of the Spring is dressed in the most beautiful flowered robe, and casts out flowers from a loose garland that she carries. The most distant lady, dressed gracefully but decorously, appears almost Madonna-like.

The Renaissance neo-Platonists saw that there could be a way of transmuting the most basic sexual desires into emotions of a higher order. They would reach first the level of ordinary love between man and woman, but would pass from there to an even more exalted state, in which the spirit of the beloved leads the man to knowledge of the divine, and to a sense of divine love no longer confined to one individual.* Venus can be seen in each of these aspects; in her association with the dance, too, we can see each of these levels at work.

There is no doubt that dance draws upon sexual energy, and that this can be used to arouse desire in others. Many a seduction has been carried out through dance. This may be a straight-forward prologue to mutual pleasure, but it can also have more sinister overtones as with the notorious case of Salome, in the Bible. Through the fascinating power of her dance she was able to achieve the granting of her wish, that the head of John the Baptist should be brought to her on a plate. The setting-up of a relationship itself is a kind of dance, although sometimes we find that our partner does not seem to be doing the same sort of steps at all! Sexual energy is a basic fuel for dance, and without it the movements would become pale and uninteresting. There is the choice to use it responsibly, which does not mean suppressing it, but, rather, knowing what you are doing with it and what the likely consequences are. There is also the choice to transform it into the next level of communication, where emotions are awoken.

An expressive gesture can convey emotion more directly than words. It speaks with immediacy, and can communicate the mood of the moment with telling simplicity. To be effective in this way, dance has to dispense with fussiness, with any move-ment that is unnecessary and which interferes with this com-munication. Most of the time our bodily communication is chaotic, sending out a number of different signals. My face may be cheerful, whereas my shoulders are drooping with tiredness and my foot tapping with impatience. In dance, all must be aligned. Body and heart become one, so that the movement itself *is* joy, sadness, or whatever. For this, far more than technique is required, and the performer must be prepared to expose herself completely to the audience.

The ultimate level, in neo-Platonic terms, has divine signifi-cance, and so relates to the sacred dance. This may not only

* See Baldesar Castiglione, *The Book of the Courtier*, 1528 (abbreviated edition in the 'Milestones of Thought' series, Frederick Ungar Publishing Co, 1959).

refer to the highly charged ritual or religious dance of priestesses, shamans and so on, but can also be present in any dance where the motivation comes from a desire to communicate truth of a spiritual order. Dances can be constructed so as to embody principles of universal understanding. The dance can also be a means of inducing religious ecstasy, as with the 'turning' dance of the dervishes, also practised in secular form in the West, where the dancer spins fast on his or her own axis, leading to a change in state of consciousness.

The Point of Stillness

I have talked about the Lady of the Dance as Venus in her three aspects of love, but yet she is one in essence, and however diverse the movements of a dance, they too must arise from a point of unity, of stillness. Eloise Ristad helped an over-paced dancer to discover this for herself :

A modern dancer showed me a difficult, fast-paced sequence of movements she was rehearsing for a concert. Halfway through she was breathing so hard I wondered if she could make it to the end ... I wasn't convinced it was endurance alone that she needed. I . . . asked her to sit down and re-run the whole dance sequence internally and find every resting point she could. 'There *aren't* any!' she objected, wondering why I was so unobservant.

'Okay, try something else first. Swing your arm out in front of you and above your head. Let it swing back down, then up, down ... Keep going with it constantly in motion.'

She tried. *What's she up to?*

'Now find out what happens each time your arm changes direction.'

Jean grinned as soon as she discovered that curious point of rest, so unmeasurable in duration, at the end of each arc. She moved her arm up, down, up ... as though the movement were a meditation, savoring each fraction of an instant of rest. She was more than ready for her assignment when she stopped ... When she had finished her first real run-through that morning she was exhausted, yet she got up silently now and danced through the whole sequence again. This time she was exhilarated and far less winded when she finished.

(Eloise Ristad, *A Soprano on Her Head*)

The Lady of the Dance

Contact with essence, the psychological equivalent of finding stillness in movement, prevents a dance – or any other performance for that matter – from becoming artificial and affected. It is the axis that the dervish dancer seeks and finds, around which everything else revolves. If this sense of unity is maintained, then techniques and conventions fall into place to serve the dance; they do not become its *raison d'être*. Just as the ancient Chinese said that music serves to enhance the silence that follows, so the dance can be said to point the way to the stillness at its centre.

The Lady of the Dance points the way to interaction – between man and woman, between music and listener. She invites an active celebration of life. The desire to dance and love of movement is not just a feminine one, although I think it would be fair to say that women have a longer and stronger association with dance than men, but the quality of that desire is feminine, and exists strongly in the psyche of women. The most beautiful and powerful dancers in myth and history are portrayed as women.

The dance of our lives is something that can be given space and permission to take place – the Merry Maidens are always willing to take another spin, if they are released from their captivity. At any age, the desire of the dance can reassert itself. In her novel, *The Fire-Dwellers*, Canadian author Margaret Laurence paints a moving, but rather sad picture of a housewife entering middle age. Restricted by a conventional marriage, she looks for excitement elsewhere, and has a brief love affair with a younger man. This satisfies some of her cravings for change, and she returns with a good will to her duties, but in her parting words says that she will not 'dance' like that again, however much she would like to. The sadness is not that she chooses her husband and family above a casual affair, but that she feels she must never visibly break out of the mould again because of the behaviour that others expect of her. Will she really be a satisfied housewife again, or will she be a 'Merry Maiden' frozen back into stone, wistfully remembering her one brief dance to freedom?

But from now on, the dancing goes on only in the head. Anything else, and it's an insult to Katie, whether or not she witnesses the performance. Well, in the head isn't such a terrible place to dance. The settings are magnificent there, anyhow. I did dance at one time, when I could. It would be a lot worse if I never had. Funny – I recall one of my mother's bridge cronies in Manawaka, and every time she came over, she'd ask my mother to put on a record, and Mother would play the old-time one with a polka on one side and a schottische on the other, and the old dame would sit there as though under heavy sedation. Maybe she was dancing in her head.

(Margaret Laurence, *The Fire-Dwellers*, Virago, 1988)

Images

Street Image

On her way to a disco, dressed up in something glittering, short and tight. In the street her hair-style and make-up look extreme, but once she gets there, she will be in her element. She's with a couple of other girls; they may meet men there, but in fact they are more eager to get into the rhythm of the dance than to form relationships. Feet are twinkling fast down the pavement, stars in their eyes as well as in the sky.

Mythic Image

The dancing maiden, who is never still, unless caught and thrown into captivity. Dancers of the stone circles, dancers of myth and history, such as the Three Graces, Salome, Isadora Duncan. All the past and present heroines of the dance in the ballroom, in musicals, ballet, Indian dance, Egyptian dance, sacred temple dances, from the bare-breasted to the silken-veiled, from ballgowns to peasant skirts. A galaxy of women dancing at all times, in all nations.

Personal Image

The itchy feet syndrome – time for a quick hop. Are you ready for a change? What of? Maybe of partners, places, careers. A delight in the actual process of change; you dance away, joyfully. Be careful, for the sober-minded do not like those who dance the changes. They call it fickle, frivolous, and say it is breaking the commandments. Can you dance your way around that?

Evolution

Youth

Young girls must dance, otherwise where else would they put all that energy? Not into fighting and scrapping, like the boys. It is difficult finding a dance that their own hearts can respond to, because those that the adults teach them may seem remote and contrived. Sometimes they pass down the dances one to another, as with skipping steps and rhymes. The older girls dance and sit around lethargically by turns; their energies fluctuate; it bewilders them, and they haven't yet learnt to handle their own rhythms.

Maturity

A woman whose interest in life is always fresh; she hasn't forgotten how to play, how to laugh at life and its trivialities. She can be gloriously irreverent. She enters the dances of her choice now; her step is light, and so is her control, so that the dance can still bubble up from inside her without repression.

Old Age

Old ladies can still be found giggling together, shocking their younger, more sober, counterparts. As they cackle it becomes apparent that we never really grow up. And yet old lady dancers can teach all of us something; the grace and carriage that can endure is stunning, the rhythm and lightness of step more meaningful at eighty than at eighteen.

Manifestations

Gifts

Welcome changes and surprises. The arrival of spring. A new hobby, friend, relationship. Gracefulness of movement. A dancing partner who encourages a boldness or beauty of movement that you never knew you possessed.

Trials

Loss of enthusiasm for life. Disapproval of others. Petty restrictions. Energy repressed by physical confinement. Big swings in energy levels, making it hard to plan ahead, or cope with events as they occur. Loss of physical suppleness and flexibility.

Rituals and Cults

Traditions of women's dances. Girls' dances and games. The means we evoke to induce a change of mood: aromas, food, fantasy, books, clothes, and so on. The etiquette of the dance floor, from formal balls to discos. The cult of women's humour.

The Vision

Of the natural flow of change, and how we may celebrate it.

Afterword

The Circle of Nine is now complete. When the circle is in place, it defines a space within it which is also an essential ingredient of the feminine psyche. Several of the chapters have given pointers to women's need to create space in their lives: the space of physical territory, space in which to think and muse, space to affirm their own outlook and intentions. The space created by the Circle of the Nine offers a place for women to discover their own personality, identity, and their commonality as women. The mythic figures that surround it are the living forces that activate, the space the place where the individual can work and reflect without intrusion. By herself, or in the company of other women, she can affirm her own sense of the feminine, making for greater awareness and confidence when she moves back into mixed society. In everyday life, time and space set apart for women to keep company together and share activities is a valuable source of strength for those involved, and various traditions have grown up in domestic, professional, spiritual and artistic contexts which provide for this.

When men and women are together, which is for most of the time in modern society, then interaction and self-expression are different. Very few of us would want to live in a society where the sexes were severely segregated, but, on the other hand, if there is no provision for single-sex activities, then it can be difficult to build up a strong sense of one's own sex, with its particular character and potential. Mythological traditions relevant to the circle of nine show one of two things. Either the circle is empty, an emblem of the male often standing outside it, just as the King Stone stands beyond the Nine Ladies stone circle in Derbyshire, or else the male figure is standing in the centre of the nine women, as Apollo among his muses, or the naked male surrounded by women dancers (see p. 5). Thus there are two models; that of the feminine enclosed, acknowledging the male, but with no other influence entering its space, and that of the feminine surrounding the male, who has come to the centre of the circle.

The book I have written is of the first type. It is about taking the feminine principles back as far as one can, and seeing them for what they are, describing them in ways that are meaningful today. A book based on the second model, of women as they are seen and known by men, and of the active dynamic between the two sexes, is another project altogether. It would come after this one, since I do not think we can really understand the essence of male–female interaction until we have some understanding of the separate qualities of each sex. Although I have made excursions into considering the relationship between men and women, and comparing the two sexes, the schema has been primarily about the feminine, the experience not only of being female, but of being a woman among other women. It is perhaps rather like an initiation ceremony, when, let us say, a girl on the threshold of womanhood might be led through a series of caves, and in each one would be shown a representation of a goddess; the stories she is told about each goddess will give form and meaning to the experiences of womanhood that await her. Myths and images presented to the young male would, in their turn, be different, and so again would those be which were told in mixed company. There are cross-overs, connections between all of these, but the form and content is different for each. The only difference with this book is that I have not written exclusively for a female readership. However, men who read it should realize that although, of course, they will find correspondences to their own experience in the material I have presented, it is nevertheless a model that is tailored to the feminine. Men may come to know some of the feminine aspects of their own character through the nine. Hopefully, they will also be willing to learn more about women too; women would welcome this.

The nine female archetypes may have considerable relevance to men, even given the fact that one could perhaps draw up equivalent male figures as parallels of the nine set out here. In what way would men and women perceive them differently? Perhaps one difference is that women feel these forces to be a part of their own being, whereas to men they are very much external figures. Think, for instance, of the tradition of the Muses; it is the male poet or artist who talks about his Muse descending, the goddess who will bring him inspiration. She is fickle, wayward and implacably demanding. He has to court her assiduously, but she will only come in her own time. For women, the Muses are already there, latent, waiting to be awoken. They are the gifts that we can give to ourselves; we can know them and call upon their presence without having to wait for an external manifestation.

The archetypes and the circle can be used dynamically when they are complete. This book has taken us to the point of recognizing each archetype individually. There are countless ways in which they can then combine and interact. There are 362,880 ways that one can make the journey around the circle, visiting each archetype in turn. Or think of the possibilities when two of the figures are put into contact; link the Weaving Mother and the Queen of the Night, for instance, and the scene is set for magic, plotting and intrigue. Introduce the Lady of the Hearth and the Just Mother and you have the potential for an epic saga of family fortunes – the dynastic touch. This is the basis from which we could construct new myth and legend, as well as being a reference for the interactions in our own lives.

As you finish your journey through this book, you may have a number of reactions to what you have read. Some ideas may have interested you or inspired you; others may have caused irritation and made you argue with points raised. My intention has not been to set out dogma, but to step into the realm of the nine female archetypes, and describe my encounters as imaginatively and as pertinently as I could. Writing this book, in itself, has been a journey, and one that, in a sense, is not finished, since each observation made opens out new fields of enquiry and question. If your own travels around the Circle of Nine have created a similar effect, then the aim of the book is at least partially fulfilled. Just as the spaces between the stones of the circle allow free access, so the realm of the archetypes is open for exploration, and each traveller will come back with her own tales to tell. It needs only to be remembered that, however strong the presence and quality of each of the nine individual figures, they all spring from one source of life, and that their difference is a celebration of the myriad ways in which this unity expresses itself in creation.

Some suggested reading

The booklist which follows is very much a personal selection; my criterion has been to choose works which I have found stimulating or useful for reference. They represent a small, but, I hope, widely varied and interesting area of that large field now known as 'women's studies'.

JANET BAKER, *Full Circle*, Penguin, 1984
A year in the life of an internationally known singer as she takes part in her last operatic productions and reflects upon her career.

JANE BOWES AND JUDITH TICK, editors, *Women Making Music – the Western Art Tradition 1150–1950*, Macmillan Press, 1986.

ANNE CAMERON, *Daughters of Copper Woman*, The Women's Press, 1984
Tales of women's mysteries and sisterhoods among American Indians.

BALDESAR CASTIGLIONE, *The Book of the Courtier*, Frederick Ungar Publishing Co, New York, 1959
An edited version of an early sixteenth-century work, notable in this context for its discussion of the conscious development of spiritual love between man and woman where a sexual relationship is out of bounds.

ANTONIA FRASER, *The Weaker Vessel – Woman's Lot in 17th Century England*, Weidenfeld & Nicolson, 1984

GEOFFREY GRIGSON, *The Goddess of Love – the Birth, Triumph, Death and Return of Aphrodite*, Quartet Books, 1978

M. ESTHER HARDING, *Women's Mysteries, Ancient and Modern*, (USA 1955) Rider & Co, 1982
A classic exploration of feminine archetypes by a Jungian psychologist.

ROBERT A. JOHNSON, *He – Understanding Masculine Psychology*, Harper and Row, 1977; *She – Understanding Feminine Psychology*, Harper and Row, 1977

Some suggested reading

SHEILA KITZINGER, *Giving Birth*, Victor Gollancz, 1971
First-hand accounts of the experience of childbirth.

ALISON LURIE, *The Language of Clothes*, Heinemann, 1981
Insights into the meaning of styles and colours that we wear.

ERICH NEUMANN, *The Great Mother*, (1955) Princeton University Press, 1972
A review and consideration of female archetypes, largely drawn from early history; the work covers far more images, in fact, than that of the Great Mother.

ELOISE RISTAD, *A Soprano on Her Head*, Real People's Press, Moab, Utah, 1982
Investigations into the problems and challenges of the performing arts.

JAMES M. ROBINSON, editor, *The Nag Hammadi Library*, E. J. Brill, Leiden, 1977
A collection of Gnostic texts, many of which describe the role of the female spirit in the Creation.

ANNE ROSS, *Pagan Celtic Britain*, Routledge & Kegan Paul, 1967

DEIRDRE SANDERS, *The Woman Book of Love and Sex*, Michael Joseph & Sphere Books, 1985
The results of a survey in which 15,000 women gave their views and experiences of sex and relationships.

PENELOPE SHUTTLE AND PETER REDGROVE, *The Wise Wound – Menstruation and Everywoman*, Penguin, 1980

ROY STRONG, *The Cult of Elizabeth*, Thames and Hudson, 1977
The image and influence of Queen Elizabeth I during her reign.

ANTONIA WHITE, *Beyond the Glass*, Virago Modern Classics, 1979
A semi-autobiographical account of a young woman's descent into insanity and her recovery.

ARKANA – NEW-AGE BOOKS FOR MIND, BODY AND SPIRIT

With over 150 titles currently in print, Arkana is the leading name in quality new-age books for mind, body and spirit. Arkana encompasses the spirituality of both East and West, ancient and new, in fiction and non-fiction. A vast range of interests is covered, including Psychology and Transformation, Health, Science and Mysticism, Women's Spirituality and Astrology.

If you would like a catalogue of Arkana books, please write to:

Arkana Marketing Department
Penguin Books Ltd
27 Wright's Lane
London W8 5TZ